ROMAN INVASION

Bran, Prince of the Carvetii
Britain, AD 84

by Jim Eldridge

Scholastic Canada Ltd.
Toronto New York London Auckland Sydney
Mexico City New Delhi Hong Kong Buenos Aires

To Lynne, my inspiration.

While the events described and some of the characters in this book may
be based on actual historical events and real people, Bran is a fictional
character, created by the author, and his story is a work of fiction.

Library and Archives Canada Cataloguing in Publication
Eldridge, Jim, 1944-
Roman invasion : Bran, Prince of the Carvetii, Britain, 84 AD / Jim
Eldridge.
(My story)
ISBN 978-1-4431-0212-4
1. Carvetii--Juvenile fiction. 2. Great Britain--History--Roman period,
55 B.C.-449 A.D.--Juvenile fiction. I. Title. II. Series: My story (Toronto, Ont.)
PZ7.E488Ro 2010   j823'.914   C2010-900165-6

First published in the UK by Scholastic Ltd., 2008
This edition published in Canada by Scholastic Canada Ltd., 2010

Text copyright © Jim Eldridge, 2008
Cover photo (background) © Bettmann/CORBIS
Cover photo of boy by Aldo Fierro
All rights reserved

6 5 4 3 2 1   Printed in Canada   121   10 11 12 13

Chapter I

The night had been pitch dark and was now turning the red and grey of just before dawn. The sun had not yet risen, but its early red streaks could be seen making patterns in the distant sky. Owls still hooted, and foxes and badgers and other creatures of the night moved through the forest, heading home before the daylight exposed them to predators of their own.

We stayed silent, hidden behind trees and concealed beneath bushes, watching as the first light of day filtered through the trees. I was with my older cousin, Carac, and five others of our Carvetii tribe. Across the track, throughout the forest, others were also hidden. More of my cousins, other warriors from our tribe. And not just men. We Britons are proud of our warrior women, who can fight hand to hand with sword or spear, the equal of any man. Our tribal leader, my mother, Queen Cardua, warrior queen, was with us. She had become leader of our tribe after my father, King Vannan, had died in battle against the Roman invaders. Now we were going to take our revenge.

1

Our spies had been keeping an eye on the Romans in their big fort and had noticed that they sent out dawn patrols to keep watch on the territory they had invaded. For the past two days the Roman patrol had travelled the same path, coming through this part of the forest. Usually it was just a party of twenty soldiers. Although we had seen the soldiers in action and knew how fiercely they could fight, our hope was that this time we would have surprise on our side. We would also have the advantage of outnumbering them. Fifty of our tribe were hidden among the trees and bushes of the wood. All of us were armed with knives, swords, axes and spears.

In the distance we heard the sound of many tramping feet. The Roman patrol was coming! I crouched behind the cover of the tree, my fist gripping the handle of my knife so tightly I thought my knuckles would lock. Beside me, Carac was holding his large axe. The others were also poised, their weapons at the ready.

Nearer and nearer came the sound of the Roman patrol, marching feet crashing down onto the earth. Then, through the leaves and branches, I saw them: a glint of the early sun catching on the metal armour the soldiers wore. Now I could see the faces of the soldiers beneath their helmets. How was it they could not see us? We were so close to them!

The soldiers at the front of the patrol began to pass us. I

felt a sickness in my stomach. This would be my first battle against the Romans. Would I be brave enough? I prayed to the goddess Brigit and to the great god Lug that I would not let my tribe down. Today I, Bran, would become a fully fledged warrior and this would be a great victory! This day the Carvetii would strike a blow for freedom against the Roman invaders!

"Aaiiiee!" It could have been the screech of a hawk or an eagle, but it was the signal from my mother for us to attack. Echoing her cry we launched ourselves from our hiding places, swords and axes and spears waving as we threw ourselves on the party of Roman soldiers. I leapt onto the back of the soldier nearest me and stabbed him hard with my knife, but the blade broke against his body armour. I threw away the knife and tried to get my arms around his neck, determined to wrestle him to the ground, but he was too strong for me. He swung his elbow back and hit me hard in the ribs, and I gritted my teeth to stop myself crying out in pain. He tried to shake me off, but I hung on grimly, still trying to use my weight to bring him to the ground. Now he had drawn his short sword and was hacking blindly at my legs, but my wolfskin leggings took the blows. Around me the battle raged, Carvetii warrior against Roman soldier, yells of war and of pain. And then the soldier took me by surprise:

he bent down suddenly and I slipped forward up his back, trying to cling on with my arms around his neck. He grabbed me and threw me with great force, and I was aware of the trunk of a tree coming fast straight at me . . . and then there was a huge pain in my head and everything went black.

Chapter II

The six of us stood as prisoners in a line: my mother, my cousins Carac, Ventius and Awyn, my eight-year-old sister, Aithne, and myself. We were in a large room in the fort where the Roman governor had his headquarters. We were chained together, iron shackles around our wrists and ankles fixed to the heavy chains. The governor sat on the high seat and looked at us. There was no anger in his face at our uprising, no rage, and neither was there any sign of respect for my mother's rank as queen. There was nothing at all in his expression, except possibly contempt for us. Behind us and to both sides stood Roman soldiers. Although their swords were in their scabbards, we knew that if one of us made a move towards the governor they would take out their swords and cut us down. Not that any such move was really possible with the weight and awkwardness of the chains and shackles that kept us held together.

My mother gestured towards my sister. "Is there any need to keep my daughter in chains?" she demanded. "She is just a child."

"Children can kill," said the governor. "We have found children as young as six years old in your armies."

"They are not in our armies," retorted my mother. "We keep our families with us wherever we go. Even to battle. Unlike you Romans, who abandon yours."

The Roman governor said nothing for a few seconds, then he answered her with a cold anger: "If you were a man, or a common warrior, I would have you killed for insulting our Roman ways. It is only out of respect for your role as a queen of the Britons that I have kept you and your kinsmen alive after your foolish attack on my troops. I have already ordered the execution of all the male warriors that we captured." For the first time he gave what might be called a smile. "You will be the queen of a tribe of women and children, Queen Cardua. All your warrior men are dead."

With that the governor got up and walked towards where my three warrior cousins, Carac, Ventius and Awyn, stood straight and defiant, and I noticed that he took care to stay at a safe distance from them.

"You three will be spared because you are, I am told, princes of your Carvetii tribe. Instead you will be sent to Rome as slaves. British princes have commanded a high price in Rome, ever since we captured your king Caractacus and sent him there in chains."

"I would rather die than be sent as a slave to serve you Romans!" spat Carac.

"I'm sure you would," nodded the governor. "And I'm sure you'll die soon enough in Rome. The circus is always in need of gladiators for entertainment."

The governor turned away from my cousins and came to stand in front of me, studying me. I scowled and glared at him to let him know he didn't frighten me. I am Bran, son of the late King Vannan and Queen Cardua of the Carvetii tribe of the Britons. We are not afraid of the Romans.

"For the boy, I have something special in mind," said the governor.

"I am not a boy!" I shouted. "I am a warrior!"

The governor looked towards my mother, shook his head and said sarcastically: "Like I said, you have children in your army."

"He is not a child!" said my mother defiantly. "Bran is a prince, raised to be a warrior like his father! He is eleven years old. Old enough to take his place on the battlefield."

"Old enough to die!" I declared.

"I am glad you think so," said the governor.

For a moment my heart stopped beating. He was going to have me killed right here in front of everyone as an example. Despite what I had said, I didn't want to die. I wanted to stay alive so that I could fight and drive the Romans out of our country. A dead Briton was one warrior fewer to fight against the Romans.

I stood up straight, my body tense, waiting for the sign from the governor for the soldiers to take out their swords and cut me down, but instead he turned away from me and walked back to stand in front of my mother.

"We are going to build a road from here in the west right across this barbarian country to our fort in the east, a distance of forty miles. Along this road we will build forts. It will mark the northern frontier of the great Roman Empire."

My mother shook her head.

"It will not happen," she said firmly. "That territory is the kingdom of the Brigantes, our sister tribe—"

"Sister tribe!" echoed the governor, and he gave a derisive laugh. "How can you call yourself a *sister* tribe to the Brigantes? The Brigante territory covers hundreds of miles, from coast to coast and from far in the south to where it borders the land of the Caledonians. The territory you Carvetii rule is barely bigger than a large farm!"

"We Carvetii have lived here for generations!" stormed my mother. "Many of us are cousins to the Brigantes . . ."

"Yes, cousins I will accept," nodded the governor. "Inferior cousins, perhaps…"

"Take off these chains and I will show you who is inferior!" shouted Ventius, and he stepped forward as if to attack the governor, but a spear was suddenly thrust towards Ventius's throat. Personally, I felt it wasn't the point of the spear pricking the skin of his throat that stopped Ventius so much as the chains and shackles that bound him to us, holding him back.

The governor gave that nasty contemptuous smile of his again.

"I wish I were going to Rome with you, Carvetii," he said. "I would quite enjoy seeing you in the circus arena against a few hungry lions."

The governor waved his hand and the soldier removed the spear point from Ventius's neck.

"As I was saying," said the governor, and he began to pace, "we are going to build a road from this point in the west right across this country to the east."

"And as I told you," said my mother as firmly as before, "the Brigantes will not allow that to happen. They will attack your forces every step of the way."

"Not if they really are your *sister* tribe," said the governor with a sneer. Pointing to me, he said, "Your son will go with the surveying engineer and the escort of soldiers as a prisoner. If the party comes under attack from the Brigantes, the soldiers will have orders to kill the boy immediately. And I will spread word of that along the line the survey party will take, so that all Brigantes from here to the east coast know what will happen to the boy if they attack. Your son, as you have just told me, is a warrior prince. No Briton will want the blood of one of their own princes on his soul."

"It will not help you!" I said loudly. "Once we are on the road I will escape and join the Brigantes in their battles against you Romans."

The governor shook his head.

"I would not advise it, my headstrong young prince," he said, "because your mother and your sister will be kept prisoner here in this fort, and if I receive word that you have escaped, then I will kill them both."

Chapter III

The next day I was taken from the room where they kept my mother, Aithne and me, and brought out into the courtyard of the fort. The chains had been taken off me, but my wrists were tied together with thick rope, and a noose had been fixed around my neck. One of the Roman soldiers held the other end of the rope as if I were a horse on a lead. The soldier gave a sharp tug, and I stumbled forward into the daylight of the fort.

Before, I'd only seen the Roman fort from the outside. It was a massive building at the top of the hill, with high walls made of timber and turf, a watchtower at each corner and smaller towers set along the tops of the walls. When I'd been brought in with my mother and the others after the battle with the Romans, I'd been unconscious. I hadn't seen anything of the inside of the fort, except the room where I woke up and the large room where the Roman governor had addressed us. Now, finally, I saw the Roman fort from the inside. The large buildings in the centre weren't round and made of wood and turf, as the buildings of our tribe were.

They were long and square and made of cloth and leather. I had heard people speaking of these buildings and saying that the Romans called them "tents." They had a sloping roof made of what looked like animal skins stretched over a long wooden pole, and then fixed to the ground with ropes. There were hundreds of these tents.

Everyone inside the fort seemed to be working: either sharpening their swords and spears, or mending something. In one area not far away from me a group of soldiers were training, practising fighting one another. I stopped to watch, but the soldier tugged again at the rope around my neck. I was jerked forward towards the gate of the fort, where an enormous line of soldiers was standing to attention, ready to leave. I stopped, stunned by the sight of so many men. There were thousands of them, all fully armed and carrying heavy packs on their backs. I had expected we would be accompanied by a troop of twenty or thirty, at most, but this huge number left me breathless. High above the column, banners and flags of different colours flew. In the middle of the column a silver eagle was held high on a pole. The soldier leading me saw the stunned expression on my face and gave a grin.

"The power of the Roman army, boy!" he said. "A Roman legion. Five thousand of the bravest and toughest warriors the world has ever seen."

I recovered my surprise and gave him a glare.

"We Britons have bigger armies than this, Roman! We have hundreds of thousands of warriors! But we do not feel the need to put them on show like this. I only stared because I have never seen so many men dressed up like puppets pretending to be warriors. A real warrior goes into battle naked and unafraid, not hiding behind a suit made of metal like a coward."

The soldier's face hardened and he raised his hand as if to strike me, but another soldier gave a sharp cough to stop him and said quietly, so as not to be heard, "Leave him till later, Simeon. Don't want to get into trouble for striking a prisoner. Especially a prince."

Simeon stopped his hand and glared at me for a moment, as if undecided about what to do. Then he brought his hand down and rubbed his cheek with it and nodded, "You're right, Asras," he said. "I'll deal with him later, when we're on the road. For now, let's dump this rubbish in the cart."

They pulled me to a cart that was about halfway along the line. I saw that there were other large wagons at the end of the line, piled with equipment, but the cart they were pulling me to was small, with a large old mare between its shafts, the big shaggy sort of horse that was used to pulling logs and heavy loads rather than the lighter, more spirited

13

horses that pulled our chariots. Sitting on the seat of the cart was a man in a short robe, with a boy of about my age next to him.

The two soldiers lifted me up, and then tossed me onto the back of the cart. It was filled with wooden stakes and I banged my knee as I hit them, but I was determined not to cry out or let them see they had hurt me. Simeon clambered up and began to tie me to the rails at the side of the cart.

"Just so you don't get any ideas about trying to run away," said Simeon, as he got down from the cart, and then he and Asras joined the column of soldiers behind it.

The man in the driving seat and the boy beside him turned to look at me. The man gave me a smile.

"Welcome, young warrior," he said. "My name is Pentheus, and this is my nephew, Talos, my assistant. We are the surveyors for the road."

I scowled back at them and turned my face away to let them know I wanted nothing to do with them. They were Romans and Romans were my enemies.

I looked towards the room where my mother and Aithne were still being kept prisoner, but there was no sign of them. The Romans were obviously keeping them under tight guard. Anyway, we had said our goodbyes already this morning, when the soldiers had come for me.

14

"The Goddess will be on your journey with you, protecting you, my son," my mother had said. "Be brave and proud."

We had hugged tightly, just in case it was the last time we should see one another. Then I had saluted her as my queen as well as my mother, kissed Aithne gently and allowed the soldiers to put the rope around my neck and take me out.

There was a shout from somewhere at the front of the line that was repeated past us down the line of soldiers, and suddenly the soldiers began stamping their feet in time, marching on the spot. The sound of five thousand pairs of heavy metal-soled boots crashing onto the earth was incredible! The soldier who had shouted out first was obviously in charge of the whole legion.

I felt the cart give a lurch, and realized the man, Pentheus, had prodded the horse into moving. The line of soldiers moved forward, with our cart trundling along in its middle. The two large gates of the entrance swung open and we left the fort and moved out into the open country, heading east. We were on our way.

Chapter IV

Even though I was angry at being taken as a hostage in this way, a part of me felt excitement. In all my life I had never been to the far east. The furthest I had been was to the mountains in the middle of the country with my mother and Carac and Awyn to meet with a king of the northern Brigantes, soon after my father died. I had heard tales about the wildernesses and forests in the east, and the magical beings who lived there, although I thought many of them to be just fairy tales told for children's amusement. Now I would be travelling beyond the mountains and would see the distant country for the first time. It was said the Caledonians sometimes roamed that far south in the eastern regions. The Caledonians were fierce warriors who lived in the north of the country. They rarely ventured to the south where we Carvetii lived. The reasons most tribes travelled were to trade or take slaves. The Caledonians only traded with their own kind in the wild mountains and valleys of the north. I had heard that they did not take slaves. In battle, they killed their enemies, and sometimes ate them. The Caledonians were a force to be feared. It was no wonder the Romans had retreated before them.

I had decided that, even though I was a prisoner, as we travelled I would find out as much as I could about the Romans and their fighting ways. The Romans had beaten us in battle time after time, even though they often had smaller forces than we did. Some of our people said the reason the Romans had beaten us so far was because they had stronger magic, or because our gods were angry with us and had deserted us. I did not believe this. I believed the Romans had beaten us because of the way they fought and their armour and weapons. I intended to find out as much as I could about the Romans so that I could pass on that information to our tribes. Perhaps we could find a way to beat them and drive them out of Britain.

As the cart rattled north over the stone road the Romans had built, towards the land of the Caledonians, I sat, tied like a dog to the rail. The rope chafed at my wrists. Although I hated to admit it, this huge number of soldiers was an awe-inspiring sight: lines of soldiers six abreast, stretching as far as the eye could see, each soldier carrying a heavy bag slung from his shoulder and armed with a spear, a sword and a shield. Then the sound of thousands of feet marching in unison as the soldier at the front chanted out the rhythm of their march, keeping them in step. With an army of this size on the march, it would be a brave or foolish warrior who launched an attack.

We only travelled about two miles north along the stone road, and then Pentheus called out something and his shout was repeated in both directions along the line, and the soldiers came to a halt.

Pentheus handed the reins to his nephew, Talos. Then he jumped down from the cart and walked forward to join the officer in charge. Pentheus began pointing ahead of us along the track, and to either side of it, and the soldier nodded. I got the impression Pentheus was giving orders, which surprised me. Pentheus had to be a very important person to give orders to a soldier who was in command of an army this large, but he did not look a bit like a warrior. He carried no weapons of any sort, although I had noticed that Talos carried a knife in a sheath hung from his belt.

The officer shouted out an order, and immediately two soldiers stepped forward to the cart and began to lift some of the wooden stakes out of the back. I tried to get in their way to hinder them, but they took no more notice of me than if I had been an insect. Pentheus had positioned himself at the eastern side of the stone road and he gestured for the two soldiers to join him there and then for them to each hammer a stake into the ground about eight paces apart. When that was done they hammered their remaining stakes into the ground at the western side of the road, so that they made a kind of double gatepost across it. Pentheus then crouched down behind one of the stakes on the western side and seemed to be lining it up with its twin on the eastern side. He stood up, satisfied, and nodded at the officer, who gave a shouted order, and one of the soldiers set off eastwards along a narrow sheep-track over the open country, carrying two more stakes. He walked for some distance, every now and then looking back towards us. He was about half a mile away when the officer raised his arm, and I saw that he was holding a flag. At this signal the soldier carrying the stakes stopped. I was baffled. It all seemed very strange.

Pentheus remained crouched down behind the stake on the western side of the road, lining it up with its twin stake on the eastern side, at the same time talking to the officer, who moved his flag to the left and right. The soldier in the distance copied the moves of the signal flag, moving first to his left, then to his right, then shuffling back to his left again, until Pentheus was satisfied. He nodded to the soldier in charge, who lowered the flag. The soldier in the distance hammered one of the stakes into the ground, and I suddenly

19

realized what was happening. This was the new road being marked out. The Romans like to build their roads in straight lines so they can move their legions along them at a fast pace. The reason for the stakes was so that Pentheus could check that this new road leading eastward would run at right angles from the existing wide north-south stone road.

The officer raised his signal flag again, and the soldier moved to the other side of the track, taking the other stake with him. Pentheus had moved to the other pair of stakes and again crouched down, using these two wooden stakes to line up the soldier in the distance. More signalling with the flag, and when Pentheus was satisfied the soldier in the distance banged his remaining stake into the earth.

Finally, two more soldiers stepped forward, each carrying a coil of thin rope. They each tied the end of his coil around the stake that marked the eastern side of the stone road and then set off to the distant posts. Once they had reached them, they looped the far ends of the ropes around the posts, pulled the ropes tight, and tied them.

Despite myself, I was impressed. It had all been done so swiftly. Just six wooden stakes and four soldiers working under the command of Pentheus, and a new stretch of road half a mile long and eight paces wide had been marked out.

Pentheus strode back to the cart, clambered up into the

driving seat and took the reins from Talos. He flapped the reins and the cart began to move forward again, turning eastwards off the stone road and onto the sheep-track, lurching more than before as the wheels creaked over the uneven ground.

Already some of the soldiers had taken picks and shovels from their packs and were starting to dig up the area that Pentheus had marked out. I realized that the reason for bringing such a huge army with us was not just to protect the surveyor but to actually build the road as we travelled.

The rest of the soldiers began to stamp their feet once more in time, their boots making the earth shudder, and then they began to march and they passed the soldiers breaking up the ground for the new road.

Chapter V

During that first day, Pentheus repeatedly stopped the cart and used the stakes and rope to make sure the road kept to a straight line and had the same width all the way along it. I remained on the cart, tied up, and looked out at the Romans as they worked, and at the countryside around us. It was country I knew well. I had played here as a small child, and hunted deer and wild boar with my cousins. Much of it was forested, especially that which ran along the banks of the rivers, but some areas were bare: moss and grass on rock and turf. And it was across this bare rocky country that the legion headed to build the road. By the time we finally stopped to make camp at the end of the day, two miles of new road were under construction behind us.

I have to admit that by the time we stopped my stomach was aching with hunger. I was still tied to the cart and had not eaten all day. At noon the Romans had stopped for a break and I saw they took some rations — they looked like biscuits and dried fruit — out of their bags to eat. Pentheus had come to the back of the cart and offered me some of his rations, but I had simply scowled and turned my head away to let him know I was not interested in touching his Roman food. He had shrugged, and he and Talos had sat down on the ground and begun eating their biscuits and fruit. It made me feel hungry and angry at the same time, but I was determined not to give in and ask them for anything. Now, as the cart jolted to a stop for the last time, I wondered if Pentheus and Talos would offer me food again. I had decided I would take it if they did, but I would not ask for it.

Talos unhitched the horse from the cart and tethered the animal with a length of rope so that it could graze but not wander off. Then, while Pentheus made a tent for shelter, Talos gathered wood and made a fire.

The Roman soldiers were busy building the perimeter for a camp, with low walls of turf and wooden stakes. I had seen them do this when they were out on patrol in Carvetii territory. If they had to stay anywhere overnight, they made a temporary camp, with defences and sentries to stop any attack; another reason why they were so hard to defeat.

Pentheus joined me at the cart. "You don't say much," he said.

I shrugged. "I am a prisoner," I said. "Prisoners don't have a lot to say."

"But prisoners need to eat. Are you hungry?"

I hesitated, then nodded.

"In that case you can come and join me and Talos by our fire and eat with us."

He pointed at the ropes that held my wrists and said: "Personally, I would have untied these ropes before now, but the soldiers argued against it. They said you were dangerous and might escape, even though your mother and sister are being held hostage. Are you dangerous?"

Inside, I felt pleased that the soldiers had said this about me, that they considered me a danger. I nodded.

"Yes," I said proudly. "I'm dangerous. I am a warrior."

Pentheus nodded in understanding, then he said: "If I untie these ropes, will you give me your word as a warrior that you will not try to escape? At least, not this evening."

I looked at the hills around us, at the way the sky overhead was darkening as the sun went down, all perfect for escape. Then I thought of my mother and sister, who would be killed if I ran away from the Roman convoy, and I nodded.

"Yes," I said. "I give my word as a warrior I will not try to escape this evening."

"Good," said Pentheus, and he began to untie the ropes. "It's easier to eat without your hands tied together. Believe me, I know."

I looked at him in surprise.

"You were a prisoner?" I asked him, shocked.

He nodded.

"Who took you prisoner?" I asked. "The Brigantes? The Caledonians?"

"The Romans," he said.

He finished untying the ropes, stepped down from the back of the cart and headed towards the small tent where Talos had got the fire going and was cooking something over it. It looked like a small joint of meat. I looked after Pentheus, stunned. He looked like a Roman. He talked like a Roman. He gave orders to Roman soldiers. Why would the Romans have taken him prisoner? And when? My head was in a whirl with this. It made no sense!

He turned to me and called out: "Well, are you coming to eat, or are you just going to sit there?"

I jumped down from the cart and joined them by the fire. This business of Pentheus being a prisoner of the Romans was a mystery I had to solve.

Chapter VI

I sat down on the grass and Pentheus handed me a wooden platter with meat and bread on it. Talos was already eating his meal, dipping his bread into the juice from the meat.

"If we are to travel together it makes sense for us to know who we are," said the man. "As I said before, though I am not sure if you were listening, my name is Pentheus. And this is Talos, my nephew and my assistant. He is learning to be a surveyor himself."

I studied Talos. Now I saw him up close he looked to be about two years older than me, about thirteen or fourteen.

"I am Bran, prince of the Carvetii," I said proudly.

"You are welcome to share our food and our fire on our journey, Bran," said Pentheus. "Is that not so, Talos?"

I looked at Talos, but he said nothing, just nodded and carried on eating his meat and bread.

Pentheus smiled.

"You must excuse Talos not speaking," he said.

"Is it because I am a Briton that he will not talk to me?" I demanded aggressively.

26

Pentheus shook his head.

"Unfortunately, Talos cannot speak in any spoken language," he said. "However, he can make himself understood. Is that not right, Talos?"

And he smiled at Talos, who nodded and used the fingers of one hand to point to his lips and then make a cutting gesture with a sideways movement.

"He has had his tongue cut out?" I asked, horrified at the thought.

Talos shook his head, spread his hands wide and shrugged in a helpless gesture.

"Possibly something happened to him when he was born. We don't know what," explained Pentheus. "But he can hear as well as anyone, possibly better than many. And he is as clever as anyone else. He knows about surveying, and providing he can draw and instruct others in what to do, he will have a good career."

I said nothing to this, just ate my food, but Talos and Pentheus must have known what I was thinking. The Romans weren't known for being caring to people with disabilities. Not unless that person was a high-born aristocrat. Talos was lucky to have someone like Pentheus looking after him and protecting him.

"You said you were a prisoner of the Romans," I said, bursting with curiosity to find out more about that. "Why?"

Pentheus shrugged.

"I am Greek. When the Romans conquered the part of Greece where I come from they took me prisoner. They discovered I was a surveyor and gave me a choice: work for them or die. I chose to live." He turned and gestured at the huge number of Roman soldiers sitting around their own campfires some distance from us. "You look at them and you see Roman soldiers because they are all dressed in the same way. The same armour, the same weapons, the same way of marching. I see men from many, many different countries." He shook his head. "The soldiers of the main legions are Roman, but most of the units are auxiliaries from Africa, Egypt, Germany, Romania, Spain, Gaul. From all over the world. They are the soldiers of conquered nations who chose to join the Roman army. As your people will do."

"Never!" I burst out defiantly. "We Britons will fight until we die rather than join with the Romans."

Pentheus gave a little half smile.

"The warriors who are prepared to fight to the death will do just that. And, when they are dead, the ones who are left will be the ones who will have second thoughts about dying. They will be given a choice: death, slavery or a life in the Roman army with freedom at the end of it. Which would you choose?"

"Death," I said proudly. "I would rather die on my feet than live on my knees."

"That is because you are young," said Pentheus. "It can be different when you have family to consider."

He looked up at the sky, and the way the light was fading around us. The hills and the trees were turning into one shade of dark and misty green.

"It is getting late," said Pentheus. "We have an early start tomorrow. We should get some sleep. You are welcome to share our tent, if you give your word not to escape."

I shook my head.

"No," I said. "Let the Romans see that I continue to be their prisoner. I don't want them to think I am soft and would seek their shelter. I will spend the night in the cart."

Pentheus and Talos exchanged looks, and Talos shrugged as if to say, "It's up to him."

"Very well," nodded Pentheus. "But I will have to tie your wrists to the rail of the cart, to keep the Romans happy."

"So be it. I am a prisoner."

Talos raised his hand above his head and waggled his fingers and pretended to shiver. Pentheus shrugged.

"As Talos says, you will be a cold and wet prisoner," he said. "The clouds indicate rain coming tonight."

29

"We Britons are used to rain," I said. "It is the way it is in our country."

"Very well," said Pentheus.

We stood up and I walked to the cart, Pentheus following. I looked back to see that Talos had collected up the wooden platters and was cleaning them with a tuft of grass. He looked at me and again mimed rain by waggling his fingers above his head, but this time he gave me a smile. He thought I was being silly and stubborn. I shrugged back at him, and gave a little nod to let him know I thought he was possibly right, but that was the way it was for me.

I clambered up into the cart and held my wrists together by the rail, and Pentheus tied them to the rail with a length of rope. Unlike the Roman soldier, he did not tie them too tightly.

"Stay here tonight without trying to get away, and tomorrow we shall only tie one of your wrists as a token gesture to the Romans," he said.

"I make no promises," I said. "I am a warrior."

"And your mother and sister are hostages," said Pentheus. "Give them a chance to live a little longer."

With that he returned to the campfire, and he and Talos put earth on the fire to put it out, and then they went into their tent.

30

I sat in the back of the cart, leaning against the side. By now it was much darker. The fires of the Roman soldiers glowed brightly in the darkness for a distance of what seemed to be half a mile. Anyone watching, waiting for the chance to attack, would see that this was a huge army. Sentries would be posted at different places along the camp. No Britons would be attacking tonight, not against an army this large. They would wait until the Romans were spread out more along the line of the new road. They would wait until the hard work of building the road had tired the Romans. At least, that is what I hoped.

As I looked along the valley at the fires and tents, I thought about what Pentheus had said about the Roman soldiers not actually being Romans, and how the Romans had spread so strongly across the whole world. I thought about Talos and wondered what had happened to stop him from speaking. And I thought about my mother and my sister, Aithne, and wondered how they were. Were the Romans looking after them? Were they being properly cared for, or were they lying somewhere with their hands bound, like me? Was the great Goddess protecting them? Was Lug ready to defend them?

The night had begun to feel cold, but I was determined to fight it. I was a Carvetii warrior. I had been raised in the cold and the wet. I had been taught how to deal with pain and suffering by the warriors in my tribe. A Carvetii boy, especially a prince, is trained to be a warrior from an early age. He is trained to hunt; to survive in open country; to use a sword and a knife and a spear. He learns to live in the forest by day and by night, to be able to track an animal or a man without being seen.

Although I was only eleven years old, I had already been through the rite of Gotha, which meant spending three days and three nights on the mountain with no weapons and nothing but a covering of animal skin. First I'd had to make a knife from stone, shaping flint against flint to give me a stone with a finely sharpened edge. Then I'd had to make a shelter and a short spear using timber from the forest.

Cunning and bravery in the face of fear — that is the way of the Carvetii warrior.

So, although I had no way to make shelter, or feed myself, I would show these Romans that a Carvetii showed courage, whatever happened to him.

I must have fallen asleep, because the next thing I remember was being woken by rain. This was not just gentle rain; this was hard, cold rain that hammered down on me, plastering my hair to my skull, sticking my clothes against my body with wet. I shifted on the wooden boards of the cart, but the ropes holding me to the rail kept me where I was. The downpour increased, soaking me through, and then I heard a squelching sound approaching the cart — someone walking over the wet grass. It was Pentheus, and he was holding a sheet of some oiled cloth, which he threw over me and then tied the edges to the rails of the cart.

"There, young warrior," he said. "Keep dry."

And then he was gone.

·

Chapter VII

The next morning it stopped raining. I expected Pentheus and Talos to pack up their tent and for us to move on again, but we didn't. Instead, as Pentheus took the oiled cloth off me, which had kept me dry through the night, and untied my wrists, he said: "We will be staying here today. I need to check that the soldiers are building the road properly. You have a choice. You can stay here, tied to the cart, or you can come with Talos and me as we make our inspection of the work."

This time I didn't hesitate before answering. Although I would have been determined to stay tied to the cart in order to show the Romans I could endure any punishment they put me through, my plan was to observe the Roman soldiers so I could report back to our own warriors about them. To go among the Roman soldiers while pretending to inspect the road-building with Pentheus and Talos would give me the perfect opportunity to spy on them.

"I'll come with you," I said.

"Good," said Pentheus. "You might even find it interesting."

The soldiers were already hard at work as the three of us walked among them. Most of them were digging, using picks and shovels to break open the ground and dig up the earth. Others were on guard duty, standing at sentry positions covering a huge area around where the road was being built. While Pentheus went to talk to one of the officers, I hung back and looked at the sentries, memorizing the kind of weapons they carried and the shape of the armour they wore.

All the soldiers looked as if they were dressed the same. Beneath their armour the cloth of their uniforms looked like it was made of wool or linen. It was dyed a deep red. I noticed they wore scarves around their necks to stop the edge of the armour from digging into their skin.

Over their red uniforms they wore vests that seemed to be made up of lots of small metal chains fixed together. I had heard this talked about as something called "chain mail," which stopped a sword going through it. On their shoulders and across their chests and backs were curved strips of metal, fixed together to make something like a half jacket. They also wore metal protectors on the front of the lower parts of their legs, and each had a metal helmet with a face guard across it.

The soldiers who were digging up the ground for the road had stripped to the waist and lain down their swords and

35

spears along with their armour and red cloth uniforms in neat piles on the ground, leaving just a dagger hanging from each soldier's belt. But those who stood on guard protecting them carried a sword hanging from the right side of the belt to match the dagger hanging from the left, and two short-handled spears. On their feet they wore leather boots.

I was committing all this to memory when there was a shout from Pentheus: "Bran! I thought you wanted to see the road!"

I hurried over to where Pentheus and Talos were standing by a deep open ditch, with Roman soldiers digging and clearing earth and stones from it.

"It's very wide," I pointed out.

"It's wide because it's an important road," explained Pentheus. "Lesser roads are only about half as wide as this one. But this road has to take a whole army right from one side of the country to the other."

The soldiers had dug a deep trench right across the width of the road. I could see it was about the depth of half a man's height.

"Why have they dug it so deep?" I asked. "The rain will fill it up and turn it into a river!"

Pentheus smiled.

"It's to stop that happening that the trench has been dug

so deeply. See there?" and he pointed to where a section of the trench had been filled at the bottom with large stones. Soldiers were walking over these stones, banging their booted feet hard upon them to tread them down. "Those large stones are to help drain the road. They are being hammered down so they will be wedged tight together."

He gestured for me to follow him, and we went to where a party of soldiers with hammers were breaking large rocks into smaller stones.

"These stones will go on top of the large stones. Then, on the very top of all of this, at ground level, we lay flat slabs of stone to give it a smooth surface. It makes it easier for men and carts to travel over."

I must have looked confused, because Talos nudged me and looked at me with his hands held out and a puzzled expression on his face.

"Talos has spotted that there is something about this that puzzles you," said Pentheus. "What is it?"

"I still don't understand why the trench has to be so deep," I said. "The soldiers will only walk on the surface of the road. Why does it need to be dug to half the height of a man? It seems a lot of work for nothing. When we Britons build a road we do it by cutting logs and laying them along a track, and that works."

"Ah, but for how long?" asked Pentheus. "After a while mud slides in between the logs and then gets stuck on top and the road vanishes. And the more a road gets used, the more that top surface gets pushed down by all those feet and those rolling wheels and the hoofs of horses, until it breaks up." He pointed at the road under construction. "This road will not break up, not for many years, no matter how many thousands of feet tramp over it. It will not drown beneath water because the rain goes through the stones right to the bottom. And we will be digging a drainage ditch along both sides of the road and filling that ditch with stones, to prevent water getting on to it." He nodded proudly. "Roads like these are why the Romans have conquered the world. Wide and straight. The Romans can move their army faster and in greater numbers than any other army in the world along these roads."

"They conquered your people with roads like these," I pointed out. "Don't you feel like a traitor?"

"A traitor to who?" asked Pentheus. "My own people are now part of the Roman Empire, as yours will be."

"Never!" I burst out.

"Fine sentiments, but that's what will happen, young warrior," said Pentheus. "That's what's happened to every other country in the world that the Romans have gone into. They are pushing their borders forward all the time."

"The Caledonians defeated them," I pointed out. "That's why the Romans are building this road, because they know they can't get any further north than here. This road marks as far as they can go."

"Not if I know the Romans," said Pentheus. "They'll build this road and put forts along it and fill them with soldiers. And when they have a big enough army gathered along this line, they'll push northwards right across the whole country. You'll see."

Chapter VIII

We spent the rest of the day camped while Pentheus walked the length of the road watching the Roman soldiers at work, making sure they dug the trench to the correct depth, checking the size of the stones that were used to fill in the trench and checking the drainage ditches at the side of the road. Talos and I went with him, and although Talos seemed interested in everything that was happening, I got bored. Once you have seen a group of men digging a hole and filling it in for half a day, there's nothing interesting to be found by watching the same thing over and over again. Also, I was more interested in finding out about the Romans.

At one point I tried to sneak away. We were walking along by the side of the road to watch yet another bunch of Romans digging and moving stones, and I hung back and pretended to be very interested in the way the soldiers trod the stones down in the trench under their feet. My plan was just to keep hanging about until Pentheus and Talos had gone a lot further on and then wander off in the other direction. If anyone wanted to know what I was up to, I would just shrug to say that I didn't understand, and then point to the cart by Pentheus's tent. But Talos was aware of what I was up to. He turned to look for me, and saw me dawdling by the side of the road, and tugged at Pentheus's sleeve. Pentheus nodded and signalled for me to join him. Inwardly I scowled, but I ambled along to where the two of them waited for me. Talos was making signs with his hands to Pentheus, touching his fingers against his hand and his arm, and touching his face, while at the same time he seemed to be making faces at Pentheus. I wondered what was going on? Was he ill? Was he having a fit of some sort? It all seemed very odd, but Pentheus seemed to take it as normal, because he nodded. As I got to them Pentheus turned and said to me: "Talos says you're bored with all this. Are you?"

I looked at Pentheus, and then at Talos, in surprise. Talos *says*? How? Talos was dumb. Was that what all that business with making signs with his hands had been about, and the funny faces he'd been making? Now I remembered that one of the expressions Talos had given to Pentheus was of someone who was miserable. Was that supposed to be me?

Talos had started making signs with his hands again: this time he made two of his fingers walk across the palm of his hand, like legs moving. Then he pointed to himself and me.

"All right," nodded Pentheus. "But only if he gives me his

41

word he won't try to escape." Turning to me, Pentheus said: "Talos suggests you and he go for a walk around the camp. Frankly, I don't think it's a good idea. But he thinks you'll be true to your word, if you give it. And it will give me a chance to get on with my work without having to keep an eye on you. What do you say?"

I looked at Talos, stunned. He had said all that to Pentheus, just by moving his hands and making faces?

I nodded quickly. This was just what I wanted! A chance to walk around the Roman camp and inspect it. To spy on the Romans!

"I give you my word," I said. "I won't try and escape today."

Pentheus looked at me, then shrugged. "I suppose your word for not escaping today is the best you can do, under the circumstances. Very well. But Talos is in charge of you. If he tells you not to do something, or not to go somewhere, you are to follow his orders. Is that clear?"

"I understand," I said. "I'll do as Talos tells me."

I still found it intriguing that we were talking as if Talos could speak. But then it struck me that, in his way, he could. Pentheus understood what Talos had "said" about me being bored. And I had understood Talos when he had suggested he and I go for a walk by using his fingers walking over the palm of his hand.

Talos gestured to me to follow him, and we walked away from the road and left Pentheus to carry on his inspections. Talos pointed towards a group of soldiers who were practising with their weapons and raised his eyebrows in a question. I was getting the hang of this. He wanted to know if I would like to watch the soldiers practise. I nodded. That was exactly what I wanted to see!

As we walked, I asked, intrigued: "How did you work out how to talk like this, with your hands and face?"

Talos shrugged and made a gesture with his hand to show a long, long way, and I knew he meant, "A long time ago. So long I can't remember."

We got near to where the soldiers were training, but a sentry wearing full armour and carrying a spear suddenly stepped in front of us and held out his hand to stop us going any further. Talos pointed towards the ground at the spot where we stood, and then held his hands wide in a questioning way. Again I noticed he used his eyebrows, making them move upwards to show a question: could we stay there and watch? The sentry hesitated, then nodded and stepped to one side so we could see the soldiers.

They were practising fighting in pairs: one holding a wooden sword, the other a length of wood in place of a spear, so they would not get seriously hurt. For this

43

practise the Romans had stripped to the waist and were fighting bare-chested.

I had already noticed that the Romans' swords were much shorter than the ones we Britons use. As I watched the Romans practise, I realized it was easier to get close to your opponent with a short sword — it looked easier to handle. A British sword is heavy and long and often has to be held with both hands and used like an axe, swinging it at your enemy. The problem is, if you miss your enemy with it, the weight of the sword swinging carries your arm onwards and leaves you open to a thrust from a spear or a slash with a sword.

I glanced across to where the Romans' weapons had been neatly laid out with their heaped clothes and noticed there was something odd about the handles of their spears. They were short and the wooden shaft appeared to be divided in two and joined together in the middle by a piece of soft metal. As I looked at the spear, puzzled by this, the reason for the joint in the shaft suddenly struck me. When a spear was thrown and hit something, whether a body or a shield, the shaft would bend at once, which meant it couldn't be thrown back at the Romans. That was very clever!

Not all of the men were practising fighting. Some were running backwards and forwards, carrying large boulders. Others were running and jumping over piles of shields while carrying their heavy bags. They were all working hard, whether they were training or practising fighting or digging the road. The only ones not hard at work were those on duty, guarding the perimeter of the Roman camp. I noticed that those on guard duty changed every so often, so that every man took his turn at digging or training or standing sentry.

I was quite surprised by the way that the Romans just let me walk about their camp. Part of me felt annoyed that they treated me with so little regard, as if I was no threat to them at all. I assumed they let me walk around free like this because I was with Talos.

"Right, boys. Time to get moving. We have work to do."

It was Pentheus, and I was startled at the quiet way he had come up behind us without my hearing him. Or perhaps my attention had been too caught up with watching the soldiers. Talos gave Pentheus a look of enquiry, and Pentheus nodded.

"Yes, the road is going to plan. I've been along the whole length of it. Now we have to prepare the next stretch, which means checking out the land. There are a few rock formations ahead that may give us some problems. Talos, you and Bran get back to our tent and start packing it up. I've got to talk to the troop commander and make arrangements. I'll join you at the cart."

45

With that Pentheus headed off in the direction of a group of soldiers who were gathered around a small table, talking and pointing at a sheet of parchment laid out on it.

Talos and I headed towards the cart. Talos pointed at the cart and the tent and mimed lifting something.

"Yes, I know," I said. "We pack up the tent together."

Talos smiled and nodded.

We were almost at the cart when suddenly there was a loud cry from about a hundred yards away to the north. We turned, and out from behind the trees and bushes rushed a party of half-naked men, their bodies painted with blue patterns, waving spears and swords, all shrieking and yelling as they ran towards us. We were under attack!

Chapter IX

The words the governor had said before we set off flashed into my mind: "If the party comes under attack from the Brigantes, the soldiers will have orders to kill the boy immediately." Surely, when there was an attack like this, the Romans would be too busy to bother with me? But I was wrong. The order had been given and the Romans had taken it to heart, because as the attackers came nearer, whooping and screaming and yelling, spears and swords waving, the sentry on duty nearest to me pulled his sword out of its scabbard and came running towards me, sword held high ready to chop me down. I went to dive out of his way, but Talos grabbed me by the arm and pulled me round behind him, and then stepped boldly in front of the advancing soldier, a hand held out palm forward to stop him, at the same time shaking his head. The soldier growled and grabbed hold of Talos and tried to throw him aside, but Talos wouldn't budge. He grabbed at the soldier's sword arm and hung on.

"No! Leave the boy!"

The cry came from Pentheus, who was running towards us.

The soldier stopped wrestling with Talos and turned angrily.

"My orders . . . !" he began.

"They are not Brigantes!" shouted Pentheus.

Just then a spear came whistling through the air and passed close over our heads.

"Quick! Get under the cart!" shouted Pentheus.

Talos and I broke into a run, heading for the cart, Pentheus running with us and urging us to go faster. The yells and shouts from the attackers were now mixed with shouts from the Romans who had rushed to join battle with them. When we got to the cart, Talos dived beneath it. As I stopped and got my breath back from the run, I looked defiantly at Pentheus.

"I will not hide!" I panted. "I am a warrior!"

"You are a prisoner!" snapped Pentheus. "Dead, you are worth nothing."

With that he pushed me roughly to the ground and forced me under the cart.

"You also gave me your word you would not escape today," he said. "Stay there, or run away and prove that the word of a British warrior prince is nothing but a lie."

With that Pentheus left us and ran to his tent. He reappeared a moment later armed with a short sword.

Talos didn't seem at all frightened. It struck me that if he'd been travelling with Pentheus and the Roman army, he must have seen plenty of battles in his life. From our position beneath the cart we couldn't see much. There were yells and screams, and the clang of metal clashing against metal and wood and leather. Every now and then I saw someone fall and a sword blade plunge downwards. There was the clatter of wood and iron as spears crashed down onto the cart, one or two sticking into the wood. Once a spear came down between the wheels and dug into the ground right next to me.

I looked out and saw Pentheus standing by the tent, sword at the ready, as a giant of a man rushed at him with a two-handed axe. Pentheus waited until the man was almost upon him and then, as the axe began its swing downwards towards him, he slid to one side and thrust the short sword forward, and the axeman ran onto the point of the sword. Blood gushed from the man's chest as he collapsed to the ground, the axe crashing down and the blade embedding itself heavily in the turf.

As suddenly as it had begun, it was all over. The attackers turned and fled back to the cover of the trees and bushes from where they'd come. I expected the Romans to go after them, but they didn't.

Pentheus bent down and called: "You can come out now," and Talos and I crawled out from under the cart.

It looked as if it had only been a small skirmish. One Roman lay on the ground, but he was moving and being attended to. I counted eight bodies of the attackers, including the axeman Pentheus had killed.

A Roman soldier came running towards us, sword still in hand. I recognized him as one of the officers.

"Pentheus!" he shouted angrily.

"What?" asked Pentheus.

The officer pointed to me.

"We had our orders," he said. "If the Britons attacked us this boy was to be killed at once."

Pentheus shook his head.

"Our orders were to kill him if the Brigantes attacked us," he said. He gestured at the dead warriors lying on the ground. "These are not Brigantes, they are Caledonians. Look at the patterns of their war paint."

The officer glared at Pentheus, incredulous.

"We were under attack and you had time to look at the paint on their bodies?!" he snarled.

"Yes," said Pentheus.

The officer stood glaring at Pentheus for a brief moment. He was still angry, but if Pentheus was right, then there was nothing he could do. Then he turned to the other Romans and shouted: "Gather up the bodies of this scum and hang them from those trees as a warning to anyone else!"

The Romans went off about their task. Talos and I walked with Pentheus towards the tent. I was still puzzled by much of what had happened, but especially by Pentheus's action. I waited until we were out of earshot of the Romans, then said: "Are you sure they were Caledonians who attacked us and not Brigantes, Pentheus?"

Pentheus shrugged.

"Does that matter? You are alive, warrior prince. Thanks to Talos."

Yes, I thought. Thanks to Talos, who had stood in the way of the soldier and had struggled with him to stop him killing me. I looked at Talos and bowed my head.

"Thank you, Talos," I said. "I owe you my life."

Talos smiled and gave one of his shrugs, with which I was getting familiar. It seemed to cover everything.

Chapter X

By early afternoon we were back on our journey eastwards. Once again Talos was sitting on the seat at the front of the cart next to Pentheus, who held the reins of the horse, and I sat in the back of the cart. However, this time I was not tied up.

Another change was that this time we only had half of the Roman soldiers marching with us. The rest were still hard at work building the road. Pentheus said the other soldiers would join us as soon as they had finished that stretch of road. Meanwhile our support of about 2,500 soldiers marched in front of and behind the cart along the line of the track.

As we moved off I looked towards the trees, where the eight bodies of the British warriors now hung from their branches like dead crows.

I was still puzzled by what Pentheus had said about the warriors being Caledonian and not Brigantes. How could he tell? The patterns that warriors preparing for battle paint themselves, with blue dye from the woad plant, do not vary greatly from tribe to tribe, only from person to person. We Britons are Celts from the great Celtic race, whether Brigante or Trinovante or Caledonian, or from across the water to the west where the Isles lie. Even more puzzling was that the Caledonian tribes live much further north, in the mountains of the high lands. The tribe immediately north of where we had been attacked was the Novantae. Either the Caledonians had come much further south than usual, or Pentheus knew more than I did about the patterns painted by warriors, or he had lied. But why would he lie? And why had Talos put his life at risk by standing between me and the soldier who had been going to kill me? This was war. The Romans were the invaders and we, the Britons, were fighting them. In a war people died. I was a British warrior. Pentheus and Talos were on the side of the Romans; so why would they side with me, their enemy, and protect me? It did not make sense.

For the next six days we continued eastwards. The days carried on in the same routine, day after day: Pentheus marked out another stretch of road and the soldiers began to dig a trench along the line and fill it with stones. I estimated that the building was going at the rate of a mile of road a day.

Sometimes more was done, sometimes less, depending on how rocky or how marshy the ground was, but it averaged a mile a day.

After a few days I accepted Pentheus's offer to share the tent with him and Talos. It was either that or be tied to the cart like a dog. Also, Talos had saved my life and it seemed to me it would be an insult to him to refuse.

In the evenings, after work had ended, we would sit around a small fire outside our tent and eat a meal that either Pentheus or Talos had prepared. Every two days Talos would go to the supply wagons at the rear of the column and return with a few vegetables and some dried meat or fish for our food. Even though I was determined to spy on the Romans so I could report back, I was glad that we did not eat with the soldiers. I owed my life to Talos, and also to Pentheus, so although I did not trust them completely, I felt comfortable talking with them as we ate. They, like me, weren't Romans. Though Pentheus and Talos worked with the Romans building this road, I felt that we shared one thing: we had all been taken prisoner by the Romans.

Pentheus told me about the country he came from, Greece, and how its culture was even older than the Romans'. According to Pentheus, the Romans had stolen many Greek ideas in engineering and science and medicine and claimed them as their own.

I, in turn, told them about my own culture, the Celtic culture, and how we are part of a race of people that stretches from the very top of Caledonia in the north, right down across Britannia to the very south and across the sea to Gaul and Spain.

One thing that fascinated me was the way that Talos joined in the conversations. He had a whole range of facial expressions: drooping the corners of his mouth to show sadness, a broad smile to show happiness, a grimace to express pain. These were combined with shrugs and shakes of his shoulders and different gestures with his hands and arms, and I found he was able to make me understand exactly what he wanted to say. Pretty soon I had forgotten that he couldn't actually speak because I knew what he was "saying," and I found myself replying to him with similar gestures of my hands and with different expressions of my face.

One evening, Pentheus and Talos told me their story.

"The Romans invaded Greece many years before I was born," said Pentheus. "But the part my family came from was on the fringes of the country and was seen as mostly harmless, so there wasn't a great Roman presence. After my older brother, Lemos, and I had finished our basic education, we were sent by our parents to Egypt to learn engineering skills. The Egyptians are some of the greatest and most

55

skilled engineers the world has ever known. The pyramids there are amazing structures; huge, and very complicated. Yet they were built thousands of years ago. The Romans, of course, had also conquered and occupied most of Egypt.

"Lemos and I did our training as engineers in Egypt for four years, and then we returned to our family in Greece. At first, things were much as they had been before. Lemos and I began to work as engineers, designing buildings for local rich people. Lemos got married to his childhood sweetheart, Mela, and they had this young rascal here."

He gestured at Talos, who grinned broadly.

Pentheus shrugged. "Whether there was something wrong with the birth that stopped Talos from speaking, we don't know. At first we just noticed that he didn't cry like other babies, and thought it must be because he was very happy and so didn't need to make a fuss. Then, as time went by, Lemos and Mela became concerned and took Talos to be examined by a doctor, who said his tongue was fine and moved well, but suggested there must be something wrong with the voice box in his throat.

"For Lemos and Mela it didn't matter, in every other aspect Talos was a perfectly normal child: irritating, annoying, always getting in the way."

Talos grinned broadly at this and laughed silently, and

made a friendly gesture towards Pentheus with his fist, as if he would get him later for those remarks.

"But what happened to Lemos and Mela?" I asked.

Pentheus sighed, and an unhappy expression came over his face.

"For some reason a few of our local politicians started saying that in our area we weren't Greek enough, there had been too much Roman influence. To be honest, it was all so much hot air. Typical politicians. They always have to be saying *something*, whether it makes sense or not. Most of the time they just give speeches to curry favour with the people they want to get money and advantages from. Unfortunately, word of what these politicians were saying spread, and the local Roman governor decided it might lead to an uprising. The Romans are quick to put down any hint of a rebellion against their rule. They sent a legion to our area and soldiers were sent out to round up suspected agitators. Unfortunately their methods were crude and brutal. Anyone they thought looked suspicious, they broke into their house and dragged them off for questioning, trying to find out who the agitators were. Of course, the real agitators were the politicians who'd started it, but most of them fled as soon as they heard the soldiers were coming.

"Unfortunately, some people used the presence of the

soldiers to settle old quarrels, or get rid of rivals. My brother and I were very successful in our business as engineers, and I think that one of our rivals used the situation to try and close us down. Someone whispered to the soldiers that Lemos was an agitator. That was all it needed. The soldiers stormed into his house to arrest him. Lemos wasn't there, so they began searching the house for him in the way that soldiers do: smashing doors, breaking open outhouses. Mela urged the soldiers to take care because of the baby, Talos, but you know what soldiers can be like. The soldiers beat her and threw her out of the house into the street.

"By this time Lemos had received word of what was happening so he hurried home. When he saw Mela lying in the road, her face bloody and bruised, he lost his temper and grabbed one of the soldiers. That was it. The soldiers killed him. Mela got to her feet and tried to stop them, but they killed her as well.

"I was out of town that day on a job in a distant village, but a messenger told me what had happened, and I hurried home. When I got there, order had been restored. The Roman commander in charge of the local troops was unhappy with what had happened because Lemos was a very respectable citizen, and he knew the whole thing had just got out of hand, but that's what sometimes happens when soldiers are in an occupying land. I was furious and told the commander I wanted the soldiers who had killed my brother and his wife charged with murder. All that did was mark me down as a troublemaker.

"I spent six months in a Roman prison. It was hard and brutal. When I came out I returned home to find that both my parents had died. I think the tragedy of the deaths of Lemos and Mela, and then my being thrown into prison, broke their hearts. All our money had gone. Talos had been taken in and cared for by some servants who had worked for my family for years.

"The Roman commander who'd had me arrested was still in charge of the troops in our area, and even though he would never admit it, he knew his soldiers had been wrong, as he'd been by sending me to prison. He knew that Lemos and I had been the best engineers in the whole area, and he offered me a deal: to work for the Romans as an engineer, or be tried for inciting a rebellion. The sentence for that was death.

"I weighed the situation up. Talos was now nearly a year old. I was his only family. The servants who were looking after him were very old, and I knew they wouldn't be able to look after him for much longer. What would happen to him once they had to give him up? Where would he go? An orphanage? And what sort of future would he have?"

Pentheus shrugged.

"I agreed to work for the Romans, as long as I could take Talos with me. Which meant they would have to provide me with a nurse for him. The commander agreed. I soon proved to him what he'd already heard: that I was a really good engineer. Word spread about my work, and I began to be moved about from area to area, wherever there was a large building project to be done. As time went on, I found myself being sent to different parts of the empire to supervise different building projects, usually the most difficult ones. And everywhere I went, I took Talos with me so that he could grow up and watch and learn to be an engineer as well, if he wanted."

Talos nodded energetically, with a happy smile on his face. Yes, he wanted to be an engineer. He mimed working, his face a grimace, and then he wiped imaginary sweat from his brow. I knew what he was saying: he would work as hard as he could, harder than anyone else, to be a good engineer. Then he slapped his hand to his chest and held up a finger, his face now proud. No, he was telling us, not just a good engineer, the *best* engineer. Number One.

"It's a good ambition." Pentheus nodded to Talos approvingly.

"Working for the Romans?" I queried.

"To be the best at what you do," replied Pentheus. Then

he yawned. "Now, after all that talking, I think we had better get some sleep. If you want to be the best, Talos, what do you have to do?"

Talos mimed going to sleep, then he opened his eyes and flapped his hands together as if they were little wings.

"Exactly," said Pentheus. "Be up with the morning birds. Get a head start while your rivals are still asleep." To me, he said: "And that's a lesson for all of us, Bran."

Chapter XI

That night, after Pentheus and Talos had told me their story, I went to the animal skin on which I slept and lay awake for a good while, thinking about the sort of childhood Talos had had. My own father had been killed by the Romans, but in battle. Talos's parents had been murdered, and then he'd lived a roaming life as he grew up, following Pentheus and the Roman legions over the whole empire. He had no home except the Roman army. Greece was just a name to him, a country far, far away in distance and in his memory. For me, this place was still my home. It was where I was born, where I had grown up among my own family and my own tribe.

As I lay there in the tent I thought of my mother and Aithne, and the story Pentheus had told about the soldiers killing Lemos and Mela to put down a rebellion. Were the soldiers near my home village doing the same thing even now? Were they going into my village and attacking and killing? Were my mother and Aithne safe?

I wished they could get a message to me in some way to let me know they were alive and well. I wanted to know that they were all right. And, if they were all right, I wanted them to know that I was safe and well and being taken care of.

That night I prayed to the god Lug to send my mother and Aithne my thoughts, and asked him to send theirs to me. A sign of some kind: an ant moving across the skin; a mouse scuttling across the tent in a particular pattern, anything so long as it was a sign to let me know they were all right and knew that I was safe. But though I lay awake for what seemed like hours waiting for a sign of some sort, none came, and eventually I fell asleep.

The next day the road building continued. As always, the soldiers worked on a rota, with different squads of soldiers engaged in different tasks. Some digging, some breaking and moving stones, some on sentry duty, and others training.

Today I noticed they weren't training in the way they had done before: exercising and practising their fighting techniques. They were practising moving in large formations, sometimes as many as a hundred men moving as one, using their shields as a huge cover over them all.

Pentheus and Talos joined me as I watched the soldiers at their practice. A group of eighty soldiers were standing rigidly to attention in what was almost a square, made up

63

of ten men one way by eight men the other. At a shout from the officer in charge, the ones in the outer ranks lifted their long shields up so that the top of the shield was at eye level, and all the soldiers inside the square placed their shields flat on top of their heads, so that together their shields made a roof. Then, at another shout from the officer, they began to move forward at speed. Another shout and they stopped.

"Impressive, isn't it?" said Pentheus beside me. "They call that movement the Tortoise."

I gave him a puzzled look at this strange word.

"Why?" I asked. "What is a tortoise?"

Pentheus picked up a stick and drew a circle in the dust of the ground.

"A tortoise is an animal that lives in a hard shell," he said, pointing to the circle on the ground. Then he used the stick to draw four legs and a head sticking out of the circle. "When danger comes, the tortoise retreats inside its shell and it's safe. Just like those soldiers inside their shell made of shields."

I looked at the soldiers practising and saw what Pentheus meant. The soldiers' shields made a protective shell over the whole group, just like that of a tortoise. Any arrows fired at them, or spears thrown, would just bounce off.

There was another shout from the officer, and this time the shields were lowered and placed in their usual defensive positions.

"The tortoise comes out of its shell," murmured Pentheus.

Another shout from the officer, and the square re-formed into a wedge shape, like the pointed head of an arrow.

"This one is the Spear," explained Pentheus.

The officer shouted another command, and the wedge of soldiers moved forwards, the men at the very front waving their swords as if they were cutting and thrusting at the enemy. The soldiers on the outer sides of the wedge behind them were also thrusting and slashing with their swords.

"The idea is that the sharp point of the spear of soldiers pushes its way into the enemy ranks, and once it's right in the heart of the enemy, it turns into the Circle," said Pentheus. "Watch."

Another shout from the officer, and now the soldiers at the side and front of the wedge began to spread out. As they did so, those soldiers inside the wedge shape moved outwards to join them, and soon they had formed a ring of soldiers, all waving their swords, with every soldier protected by his shield.

"The Circle is perfect for defence and attack. Because it's

a closed circle, the enemy can't attack the Roman soldiers at their backs. And the Circle can move forward, further and further into the enemy's ranks. If one of the soldiers in the Circle is killed, the Circle just closes up and becomes a bit smaller. Now, imagine not just one wedge-shape that turns into a circle, but a line of such wedges. When they join up, it's a strong line of attack that can't be defended against. And there will be other wedge-shaped formations of soldiers behind those at the front.

"Bear in mind that the enemy's best and strongest warriors are usually in the front of their battle lines. Isn't that so?"

I nodded. That was the way it was with us Britons; our bravest and strongest in the front to give heart to the others.

"So just think about that, Bran. Once the enemy front line has been killed or run away, what will happen to the enemy further back?"

"They will die or flee," I admitted.

"Now do you see how the Romans always win, whatever the opposition?" said Pentheus. "The real power the Romans have is in the way they organize their soldiers. Battle formations like the Tortoise and the Spear and the Circle. And they only succeed because of the Romans' powerful military discipline. Soldiers obey orders at all times, even if it means they will die. There is no power on earth that can defeat them."

"The Caledonians did," I pointed out. "They drove the Romans back. That is why you're building this road as the last line of defence."

Pentheus smiled.

"Ah yes," he said. "The Caledonians. But they didn't beat the Romans because they were stronger and more organized. The landscape beat the Romans in Caledonia, in the mountains, the wooded valleys, the bogs and marshes. That, and the fact that the Caledonians outnumbered them."

"We Britons outnumber the Romans here," I insisted.

"But not by enough," said Pentheus. "And you Brigantes are not as fierce as the Caledonians. The Caledonians are like wild animals. And they know their own country, their mountains with their secret trackways and their thick dark forests, and they can disappear in them without trace." He shook his head ruefully. "No, the Romans have already got their hold on your country, young warrior. This road will be the final nail in your people's coffin."

Chapter XII

After a few days the soldiers we had left behind working on the first stretch of road joined us and began work on yet another stretch of road that Pentheus had marked out. And so it went on, day after day. After twelve days about thirteen miles of road had been completed.

"And here," said Pentheus, "the soldiers will build the first fort along this road."

Talos shook his head and held up two fingers, then pointed back the way we had come. Pentheus laughed.

"Of course, Talos is correct. This will be the *second* fort. The first already exists at Lugavalium, where we began our journey. But we don't need to be involved, not at this stage. This fort will be built out of timber and earth. The soldiers will cut down trees to make the walls and pile up earth inside and out as protection. The ditches made around the outside of the fort from the digging will also be a line of defence. Later, when the governor decides to have the fort strengthened and made out of stone, then, perhaps, Talos and I will return and supervise the work. But for the moment, the soldiers don't need our expertise. They know what they are doing: every Roman fort is built in the same way. Some forts are bigger, some are smaller, but the basic design remains the same. Wooden stakes for the outer walls with watchtowers along them. They'll build it quickly enough. Our task is the construction of the road."

I looked around at the open countryside, curious.

"Why build the fort here?" I asked. "There are no Brigante camps nearby to protect against. Or Caledonian."

"The Romans build their forts a day's march apart, which is about thirteen miles," said Pentheus. "That way a troop of soldiers will always have shelter and protection overnight, wherever they might be along the road. After another thirteen or so miles of road have been made, they will build another fort. The next fort along the road after that will be the one they've already built in the east at Coriosopitum. So this road will have four forts along it, one at each end and two in the middle. And later the Romans will add more forts in between those. I suppose we could build smaller forts at closer intervals along the way, but our main purpose is to get this road finished as quickly as possible."

We left a party of soldiers marking out the area the fort

would cover, and cutting down trees to make the wooden walls, and continued on our way east with the rest of the soldiers.

I had thought that the road would continue in a straight line the whole way, but I was wrong. When Pentheus came upon a particularly large area of rocky cliffs in the way of the road, he moved the road so that it bent around them. I noticed that he made the course of the road move some distance away from the cliffs in a wide arc.

"The governor wants this road built quickly," he explained to me. "We could spend weeks, maybe months, breaking a way through those cliffs. Much quicker to go round them."

"But you've made the road longer by building it further away from the cliffs," I pointed out. "Why didn't you run it alongside the cliffs? That would have made the road shorter and saved you time building it."

"To prevent an ambush," said Pentheus. "The army likes to see where it's going and what's ahead. Anyone trying to ambush the army as they walk along this road will have to run over open ground."

As the time passed I began to respect Pentheus's skill as a surveyor and builder. The road he was building would last a very long time. And there was no obstacle he came to that would stop the stone road. We came to a river. My people would have built a wooden bridge across it, wide enough to take a cart, but only a light cart. Pentheus needed a bridge that would take the weight and strain of thousands of armoured men, as well as their wagons and horses crossing it, and for this he was going to build it in stone.

He set the men to digging large stones out of the ground and shaping them into squared blocks with hammers and chisels. While some were doing this, others built a frame for the bridge out of wooden poles tied together.

Pentheus had soldiers hauling rocks from the surrounding area to the river and rolling them into the water, where they were boxed in with lengths of wood cut from nearby trees. Then he got them to mix lime dust with water from the river and pour it into the boxes of rocks. In this way he built a series of solid platforms of rock and cement, with channels in between the platforms so the river could still run its course. Once he had done that, he put the men to work building columns of the cut stone blocks on these rock platforms that would support the bridge.

To build the round arches that would support the stone road over the bridge, he had patterns made of wood that looked like big mushrooms with round tops, and they were pushed into place in the spaces between the tops of the supporting columns. Then large stones were cut into wedge shapes, and these were put on top of the wooden mushrooms

71

and hammered into place. When the wooden patterns were taken away, the wedges of stone stayed in place, trapped together by their weight and shape.

The whole structure was cemented to make sure it wouldn't fall down when the strong rains came. Finally flat stones were laid across it from one side to the other. The stone bridge took time to build, but when it was finished it was very strong and very impressive. I realized what Pentheus had meant when he said that nothing could stop the Romans. Not cliffs, not rivers. And so far the only warriors who had beaten them had been the Caledonians. But Pentheus had told me that the Romans would not accept defeat by the Caledonians. Once this road was finished, they would attack the Caledonians again. And again. And again, until the whole island of Britain was under Roman rule. But I knew that would never happen. First they had to enslave my own tribe, the Brigantes, and as long as I was alive that wouldn't happen. Even if I were the last Brigante warrior left alive, I would fight the Romans as a free Briton. The Romans would never win.

Chapter XIII

Day after day we continued, heading ever eastwards, across the bleak mountains. Up there the winds were sharp and cold the whole year round, and they blew the few trees that grew there so hard they looked strange and twisted and bent. Some said that this land was cursed by the Goddess and it was a land where only the dead walked, but that didn't stop the Romans. Whatever obstacle we came upon, rock or river or valley, or cursed land, the road continued. I had seen so much road being made in the same way, day after day, that I was sure I could build a road like that in my sleep.

Always, the soldiers worked: those who had finished their section of road far behind us caught up and then began working on a new section. It was the same with those who had built the fort: a thousand men had been left to guard the fort, while the rest marched at speed along the new road, joined us, and set to work again. By the close of the twentieth day of our journey nearly twenty miles of road had been finished, with one fort built. The road was half completed. With a thousand men still working on the road and yet to catch us up, and another thousand guarding the fort, it meant our travelling expedition was now down to three thousand soldiers.

In all that time there had only been one attack by British warriors. I wondered if this was because of my presence, because word had spread that a prince of the Carvetii was being held hostage and he would be killed if the Romans were attacked. The governor seemed certain that keeping me hostage would stop the Brigantes, but I wasn't so sure. The truth was, although we Brigantes were all one people, there were many sub-divisions, and not all of the smaller tribes agreed with one another. Over the years I had heard of many battles taking place between different sections of the Brigante tribe. Sometimes, the battles were over who owned a particular section of land, sometimes they were feuds between different families. Not all tribes did as they were told by the king of the Brigantes. These squabbles often meant that one branch of the tribe could take it into their heads to ignore any orders sent out by the king of the Brigantes and do exactly what they wanted. And if a group of them felt like attacking the Romans, then they would. My own feeling was that the only thing that had prevented them launching a second attack so far was the size of the Roman force. But if they could find a way to get past the Roman defences, then they would.

I was soon to be proved right. As I was dropping off to sleep in Pentheus's tent on the twentieth night of our journey, a sudden shouting and yelling from outside brought me wide awake. I recognized the sound: war cries from the Brigantes. The Brigantes were attacking the Roman camp!

I leapt to my feet and rushed out of the tent to see what was going on. Talos and Pentheus were close behind me.

Outside, the darkness was barely lit by the glowing of dying fires, left over after mealtime. It was difficult to see clearly, but every now and then metal caught the reflection of the fire glow. One thing I could see: the area around our tent was a scene of chaos: Roman soldiers, some in armour, some in their shirts, battling hand to hand with fully armed Brigantes.

The Brigante warriors had somehow managed to breach the Roman sentry lines. My guess was they had crawled slowly on their bellies, keeping low and quiet, stopping whenever a sentry moved. They would have kept watch on the sentries during the day, watching out for the one who seemed the laziest, or the one who seemed cold and wasn't paying as much attention as he should. My cousin Carac had told me there were always men like that in any army. He called them "the weak link." If there were sentries like that on guard duty, then they were the ones to target when making a silent attack.

Now the Brigante warriors were inside the Roman defences, waving their swords and spears, shouting and yelling as warriors do to frighten the enemy and put them off balance. Already bodies lay on the ground, both Roman and Brigante, some dead, some wounded, some dying.

Suddenly I was aware of a movement behind me, and I spun round in time to see a Brigante warrior swing his axe at Pentheus, who managed to dodge to one side and escape most of the blow, but the axe glanced off his arm and Pentheus fell backwards against our tent, blood gushing from his wound.

The Brigante then swung round towards Talos, and hit him on the head with the handle of his axe, and Talos crumpled to the ground. The warrior swung the axe back over his head ready to chop it down on Talos. I yelled out "No! Stop!" in our own language, but I could see by the crazed look in the warrior's eyes that he had been overtaken by blood lust, a madness that grips some warriors deep in battle. Desperate to save Talos, I snatched up the nearest long object I could see lying on the ground, a spear, and, as the warrior swung his axe, I jerked it towards him to try and ward off the blow, or put him off balance so that he would miss. The warrior must have seen it coming out of the corner of his eye because he tried to twist away from it, but instead the force of his axe-swing made him fall forwards, and the next second the point of the spear had gone right into his throat.

The warrior gave a terrifying gurgle and blood gushed out of his mouth and nose. His eyes rolled, the axe dropped from his hands and he waved his hands in the air in front of him, as if trying to grip something, and then he crashed to the ground, the force of his fall tearing the spear handle from my grasp and pushing the point of the spear right through his neck and out the other side.

I was shocked. I had killed one of my own warriors! I began to tremble as I looked down at him. He was huge lying there on the grass, staring up at the night sky with wide-open sightless eyes, the spear right through his neck.

I felt a tug at my arm. It was Talos, standing and swaying slightly, blood trickling down his face from where the axe handle had hit him. He pointed, and I looked and saw Pentheus sitting on the ground, desperately trying to stop the flow of blood from the gaping wound in his arm, but not able to do it properly with one hand.

I gestured at Pentheus and the tent to Talos, and he nodded. Then he and I grabbed Pentheus under his arms and dragged him inside the tent. Once inside I picked up a strip of leather, wrapped it around Pentheus's upper arm and tied it tight, and then pushed a piece of wood through and began to twist it to cut off the flow of blood to the wound. When it was as tight as it could be, I took a bag of water and began to wash the blood away from the wound. The axe head had opened up the skin and the muscles beneath, but it hadn't broken the bone.

I was looking around for something to tie around the wound to close it, when Talos stopped me. He pointed at himself, then at Pentheus's wounded arm, and put his two hands together, knitting the fingers together to say, "I'll mend it."

I nodded and moved away. I was still feeling sick at what I had just done. To kill a Roman was one thing, but to kill one of my own Brigante warriors . . ! I felt a burning sense of shame and guilt. Every Brigante would know what I had done. I would be an outcast! The Goddess would punish me! My soul would be forever torn to pieces by eagles!

Outside the tent the battle still carried on, but more distant now. The warriors near to us had been beaten, but there were still skirmishes going on elsewhere in the camp.

I tried to take my mind off the warrior I had killed by watching Talos at work on Pentheus's wound. He had taken big cloves of garlic and was crushing them into a bowl. Then he gave Pentheus a piece of wood. Pentheus looked

78

at the bowl, then he nodded and put the wood between his teeth. I realized that Talos was going to pour the juice from the crushed garlic onto the open wound, and I knew for Pentheus it would feel like having his arm set on fire. Talos poured the garlic juice over and along the open wound, and Pentheus groaned and bit down on the wood to stop him from biting through his tongue as he clenched his teeth against the pain.

Then Talos spread the paste from the crushed garlic into and around the wound. Sweat poured from Pentheus's face with the pain he was suffering.

After he'd finished applying the garlic, Talos went to a bag near his bed and took out some large dried leaves. He put these along the length of the wound and began to bind the wound together with strips of clean white cloth. When that was done, he put another clean cloth over the whole wound and tied it into place. Already blood was starting to come through the cloth and stain it red, but Talos seemed satisfied.

Pentheus had stopped biting on the wood now and spat it out. Then he looked at his arm, and patted Talos on the shoulder, forcing a smile as he did so. It was then he saw for the first time the blood on Talos's face. He gave a start and reached out towards Talos, but Talos stopped his hand

and shook his head. He took a cloth and wiped the blood from his face, and both Pentheus and I could see that it had been nothing major, just a small cut high on Talos's forehead that had bled a lot, making it look worse than it was.

With Pentheus and Talos safe, I stumbled out of the tent. I didn't want to, but I had to look at the Brigante warrior again. I think I was hoping that he wouldn't be dead, that he would have got up and walked away, but he was still in the same position, his arms flung wide, his eyes still open, the spear still through his neck, blood on his face, dead; and I knew that I was cursed for ever.

Chapter XIV

Remembering what had happened before, when Talos had saved me from the Roman soldier during the previous attack, I expected the Romans to come to kill me. After all, those were the orders that the governor had given. I left the tent, went to the cart, climbed on to it and sat and waited for the Romans to take me. I knew that death was to be my punishment for killing the British warrior. Not punishment by the Romans, but by the goddess Brigit or the god Lug for what I had done; the Romans would just be the instruments carrying out the will of the gods.

Around me in the dim glow of the campfires I saw the Roman soldiers clearing up after the attack, removing the bodies of the dead, both Roman and British. The Roman bodies were laid neatly and gently side by side, while those of the British were piled one on top of the other like so much rubbish, and among them was the body of the British warrior I had killed.

After a long time, the officer in charge of the soldiers arrived and went into the tent. I assumed he was talking to

Pentheus and explaining that they knew this had been an attack by Brigantes, and so I had to die. I also knew that this time there was nothing Pentheus could do to save me.

The officer was only in the tent for a short while and then he came out with Pentheus and Talos. I expected them all to come to me in the cart, but instead the officer walked away. Pentheus and Talos joined me at the cart.

"I am to die?" I asked.

"One day," said Pentheus, "but not today."

I was puzzled.

"But the orders of the governor . . ." I began.

"I told the officer you had killed a Briton to save our lives. I wasn't the only one who saw you do it. So did two of the soldiers. The officer in charge says because of what you did, you are reprieved. You will not die. For a while, anyway."

I stared at him, stunned.

"They are not going to kill me?"

Pentheus shook his head.

"No," he said.

"But I have to die!" I said. "It is my punishment for what I did!"

"You saved Talos's life," said Pentheus.

By his side, Talos nodded. They both looked puzzled at my words.

"You do not understand . . ." I began.

Pentheus interrupted me.

"No," he said, "I do not understand. And at this moment I do not have the energy to listen to you and try to understand. I thought you would be pleased." He gestured at his wounded arm and at Talos. "We have to rest tonight because there is work to be done tomorrow. We will talk in the morning." He pointed at the tent. "Are you coming into the tent?"

I shook my head.

"I have to wait here for my punishment," I said. "It is the will of the gods."

Pentheus looked as if he were going to argue with me and insist I go into the tent for shelter. Then he shrugged.

"Very well," he said. "Stay here then. We will talk in the morning."

Then he and Talos headed back to the tent.

I sat on the cart and watched the soldiers finish clearing up, and then some took guard duty while the rest settled down to sleep for a few hours. My heart was heavy. I had committed a sin, one for which I should have died. And yet I was still alive. Was this to be part of my punishment: the torture of waiting? Or would the Goddess send her messengers tonight to kill me? And if so, what form would they take? Would it be eagles? Lightning? Wolves?

That night I hardly slept. I dozed for a few moments, but kept waking, listening out for the sounds of the messengers of my death. But, to my surprise, I did not die that night. As dawn rose the next day, Pentheus came out of the tent and joined me at the cart.

"How are you this morning, Bran?" he asked.

"I am cursed," I said. "I am waiting for the Goddess to send her messengers to kill me and carry my soul to hell for what I have done. I killed a British warrior."

"Yes," said Pentheus. "So you said last night."

He pulled himself up onto the body of the cart. I noticed that he winced as he did so from the pain in his wounded arm.

"You are not to blame," he said. "This is war. What you did happens in war."

"No!" I said. "War is killing your enemy. That is good. I killed one of my own warriors!"

"You saved Talos's life," said Pentheus.

"But the blood of a British warrior is on my hands. I am cursed and will die for what I did."

"You did not do it on purpose," said Pentheus. "It was an accident. I saw what happened while I was trying to stop my bleeding. It looked to me that you were just using the spear to try to stop him from killing Talos and he fell onto it."

"That does not matter," I said. "I killed one of my own. You do not understand. You are not a Briton. You do not know of our gods and goddesses."

Pentheus gave a sort of smile.

"I am a Greek," he said. "We Greeks know all about gods and goddesses. Our history is filled with them. Some vengeful, some caring. Everyone has gods."

"But ours are true gods," I said. "Ours have the power of life and death."

Pentheus looked as if he were about to correct me, but then he saw the real pain I was in, and instead he said gently: "Tell me about this power."

And so I told him. I told him about the Goddess, Brigit, who was the Mother of us all and who had given us the name of our tribe, Brigante, after her own name. "To kill a Brigante is to kill one of Brigit's children!"

"But you Brigante are always fighting and killing one another," said Pentheus. "In all the time the Romans have been here, I have known it. Fighting for power, or for revenge, Brigante warriors kill other Brigante warriors."

"But not for the Romans!" I insisted.

"You did not kill that warrior for the Romans," countered Pentheus. "You killed him accidentally while saving Talos's life. And you did it because you owed Talos your life after he saved you from the Roman who was going to kill you."

I shook my head.

"I hear your words, and they seem to make sense," I said. "But in my heart I know I have offended the Goddess. And Lug."

"Lug?" asked Pentheus.

I told him about the great god Lug, who had particular power for the Britons in our area.

"Even the Romans believe in Lug! After all, they named the largest fort they built here in our land Lugavalium in his honour!"

"The Romans honour nothing but the Roman way," said Pentheus. "They called that fort Lugavalium to try to make it holy to the Brigantes in an attempt to stop your people attacking it. Believe me, the Romans cannot be trusted when it comes to gods. They steal gods from other people and try and make them Roman by giving them Roman names. They did it with our Greek gods. After they had conquered us, they stole our gods and gave them Roman names. Zeus became Jupiter. Poseidon became Neptune. The goddess Hera became Juno, and so on."

"Why would they do that?" I asked.

"So that everything in the whole world becomes Roman

in some way or other," said Pentheus. "I told you before, the Romans have become the rulers of the world, but not just because they have the biggest and strongest army. With every nation they conquer, they take the parts they like and made them Roman, and then they destroy the parts they disapprove of. In this way they intend to make the whole world, and everyone in it, Roman. And those who aren't Roman will be brushed aside."

I thought about what Pentheus had said about the Greek gods and asked him: "If the Romans steal gods and goddesses, then they don't really believe in them? They don't believe that gods and goddesses have powers?"

"Oh they believe all right," said Pentheus. "There are temples to Apollo and Mercury and the others in Rome, and Romans will make offerings to their chosen god or goddess. But if one particular god lets them down, they'll switch to another one." Then he looked around to make sure no soldiers were in earshot. Even then he lowered his voice as he said: "Except for the soldiers. They have only one god, but they are very secret about him. They don't like anyone else even knowing about the fact they worship him."

"Why?"

Pentheus shrugged.

"It's to do with having power. The soldiers of the army are

all supposed to swear allegiance to the Emperor, to die for him if necessary. But, in truth, the army has killed emperors it did not like, especially if it thought that emperor was a threat to its power. The true loyalty of all Roman soldiers is to the army. And so they have their own god of the army who is more important to them than any emperor. So, even if they kill an emperor, or any other ruler, they won't have offended their own god."

"Who is their own god?" I asked.

Pentheus looked around again to make sure that no one was listening, and then whispered, "Mithras."

"But why is he so secret?"

"To prevent the Emperor or the politicians from taking him over as theirs. Only soldiers can be disciples of Mithras. And I warn you, Bran, do not speak his name when soldiers are around or they will kill you for committing sacrilege. And not I, nor Talos, nor even the Emperor himself could save you."

Chapter XV

After Pentheus had left me, I remained sitting on the cart and waited for my punishment. Despite all Pentheus's words, I still knew in my heart that what I had done was wrong and I would pay for it. Pentheus and Talos left me alone. The morning passed, and no punishment happened. No fierce bird came and pecked my eyes out. No animal came from the woods to kill me.

It will come later, I told myself.

The Roman soldiers continued with their work building the road, and Pentheus and Talos fussed around watching them, Talos making marks on a wax tablet at things Pentheus said to him.

Then, just after midday, there was the sound of a trumpet being blown and immediately the soldiers laid down their tools and began to form into lines. Within a few moments they had formed an enormous square, all facing towards the centre. Pentheus and Talos came to the cart and joined me.

"Come down from the cart," said Pentheus. "We have to move away, out of sight. We'll walk back and join the stores wagons."

"Why?" I asked, puzzled.

"I'll tell you as we walk," said Pentheus.

I climbed down from the back of the cart and then walked with Pentheus and Talos towards where the wagons with the stores were gathered at the edge of the camp.

"They have identified the duty sentry whose laxness last night let the warriors into the camp," said Pentheus. "He fell asleep while on guard. He is going to be punished. But the punishment can only be witnessed by other soldiers. It's a military matter. We are civilians. They don't want us involved."

"What kind of punishment?" I asked.

Talos mimed using a whip.

"Whipping?" I said.

Talos and Pentheus both nodded.

"But a whipping is nothing," I said. "A couple of lashes. Why is it a secret kept only for the soldiers?"

As I spoke the trumpet sounded again, and two soldiers appeared from the tents, walking stiffly, their eyes fixed ahead. Between them marched a soldier, but stripped of his uniform; he was barefoot and dressed only in a loincloth. But still he marched like a warrior, stamping his bare feet down in time with the soldiers on either side of him. As they passed us and headed for the square of soldiers, it hit me with a shock that I recognized him.

"That's one of the soldiers who put me in the cart," I whispered to Pentheus.

"We must hurry," said Pentheus. "The soldiers will not take kindly to us being here when the punishment is carried out."

As we hurried along towards the wagons I tried to remember the soldier's name. Asry . . . something. No, Asras. That was it. Simeon and Asras, they had called one another. And now one of them, Asras, was about to be punished. But what sort of punishment was it that was for a soldier's eyes only?

We reached the stores wagons and climbed into the back of one.

"There," said Pentheus. "Now there is no chance of us giving any offence."

"Why this secrecy?" I persisted.

"It is not secrecy as such," said Pentheus. "More about military pride. The soldiers don't want civilians witnessing the punishment in case the soldier disgraces himself by begging for mercy."

"What is the punishment?" I asked again. "You said it was a whipping?"

Pentheus nodded. "Yes," he said. "A hundred lashes."

I looked at them both in horror.

"A hundred? But that will kill him!"

"Possibly," said Pentheus. "If so, whether Mithras takes his soul will depend on how bravely he dies." He sighed. "Roman discipline. It's what drives the army ever forward. Fear of their own commanders has to be greater than their fear of the enemy." He shook his head in disgust. "And they call you people barbarians."

We sat in the store wagon and waited. Outside there was silence. No sound of yells from Asras, no sound from the soldiers. Finally, after what seemed like ages, we heard the trumpet again.

"It's over," said Pentheus.

He got down from the store wagon and Talos and I followed him, and we headed back towards our own tent.

The soldiers had now been dismissed from the square and were going about their tasks as before. But I noticed that their manner was quiet and subdued, their faces stony. They didn't talk to one another. As we neared our tent I realized the reason for this atmosphere: four soldiers were carrying a stretcher. On the stretcher was a red cloak covering the body of a man. One bare foot dangled from beneath the red cloak. Asras hadn't survived the punishment.

The rest of that day the Roman soldiers went about their

work. I remained on the cart, waiting for Brigit or Lug to send my punishment for what I had done, but none came.

At the end of the working day I refused the food that Pentheus offered me and remained on the cart. If Brigit and Lug wouldn't punish me, then I would punish myself. I would not eat. And when night came, I told Pentheus and Talos that I would spend the night on the cart rather than join them in the tent. I wanted it to storm. I wanted the gods of rain and lightning to send me my punishment for what I had done, but that night the sky remained clear and cool.

After what seemed like hours of sitting on the cart, waiting for the worst to happen, I felt my eyes grow heavy with tiredness. I was drifting off to sleep when a hand shook me. I guessed it was Pentheus, come to try to persuade me to sleep in the tent.

"No, Pentheus," I said. "I must stay here."

"But not for much longer, you British scum!" snarled a low voice.

I opened my eyes, startled, and found myself looking into the angry face of Simeon, the Roman soldier. He was holding a knife pointed straight at my throat.

"My brother was killed today because of you!" he grated. "Whipped like a dog."

"Asras," I said.

Simeon glared at me, the anger in his eyes burning like hot coals.

"You dare to speak his name!" he spat. "My wonderful older brother! One of the truest and bravest men I have ever known. He brought me up and looked after me our whole lives! He had been working on this road for days on end, working harder than any other man, barely taking rest. That's why he fell asleep for a few seconds. That was all. A few seconds! It could have happened to any man. It could have happened to me. But it happened to the best man who ever lived. And all because of you British dogs. Well, I'll have my revenge, scum!"

"Simeon!"

A shout behind him made him turn. Two other soldiers had appeared, and they rushed forward and grabbed him, pulling him away from me.

"What are you doing?" demanded one angrily.

"Claiming blood vengeance!" snapped Simeon, struggling to break free of their grip, but they held him too firmly.

"And if he dies, what will happen to us?" said the other. "Decimation!"

"No!" shouted Simeon angrily.

"Yes!" insisted the other soldier.

The commotion had obviously woken Pentheus and Talos, because they came out of the tent and looked at the three struggling soldiers, and at me in the back of the cart.

"What is going on?" demanded Pentheus angrily. "What is all this row? Do you want me to call your commander?"

This seemed to bring Simeon to his senses, and he stopped struggling, but continued to glare at me.

"I'm afraid he is a bit confused," said one soldier, apologetically.

"Too much to drink," added the other. "He didn't mean anything."

We watched the two soldiers take Simeon by the arm and lead him away, back to their tents. I knew the bit about Simeon having had too much to drink was a lie. He had been close to me and I had smelt no drink on his breath. It had been anger and hatred, pure and simple.

Talos looked at me and spread his hands wide, questioningly. I shook my head. I didn't feel like talking about what had just happened. Talos gestured at the tent and made that face he always did, asking a question: did I want to go inside the tent?

Pentheus nodded. "A good thought, Talos," he said. Turning to me he added: "In case it happens again."

I shook my head.

"No," I said. "He was the brother of the soldier who died today. He was made mad with grief. Unless Asras had other brothers in the legion, I think I will be safe tonight."

Pentheus looked as if he were about to argue, but then he shrugged.

"Very well," he said. "We'll talk about it in the morning." Turning to Talos, he said: "Come, Talos. You and I need our sleep. We have a long day's work tomorrow."

Chapter XVI

After Pentheus and Talos had gone back into the tent, I sat on the cart and thought about Simeon. I knew that wasn't the end of it. I could tell by the anger in his eyes. He would try again, and the next time he might succeed. In one way I was relieved: I knew now what was to be my punishment. Instead of a wild animal to tear me to pieces or lightning to strike me dead, the Goddess had sent a Roman soldier to kill me after all.

I must have finally fallen asleep because I found myself being shaken awake by Pentheus.

"How do you feel, young warrior?" he asked with a smile, trying to cheer me up. "See, it is dawn and you are still alive. Your gods have decided to let you live after all."

I forced a smile back at him, even though I didn't believe it. Suddenly, I blurted out: "Pentheus, what does 'decimation' mean?" The word the soldier had uttered had been puzzling me all night.

Pentheus frowned.

"Where did you hear that word?" he asked.

"Last night," I said. "When Simeon was here, one of the soldiers told him to leave me alone. He said if he didn't they'd suffer something called 'decimation.'"

Pentheus nodded.

"He could well be right," he said. "You are a hostage by order of the governor. That means you are to be kept alive so the road can go through. If a Roman soldier killed you — except under orders, that is — then that could be seen as an offence against the governor, which would be treason. And treason and mutiny in a legion are usually punished by decimation. Decimation means killing every tenth man. It happens if there is suspicion of rebellion or mutiny fermenting in a legion. Every tenth man is executed."

I looked at him, shocked.

"But in a legion of five thousand men . . ."

Pentheus nodded.

"Yes, the Romans will kill five hundred of their own soldiers without hesitation, if they think it will keep the others in line. As I said before, the Romans rule by fear."

Talos had now appeared beside the cart and clapped his hands together, and then he gestured towards the distant east. He had an impatient look on his face.

"Yes, quite right, Talos," smiled Pentheus. "I have been talking too long." To me he said, "We are moving on from this place this morning. We have a road to build, remember. So, once we have eaten, you can give Talos a hand packing our things up and putting them onto the cart, and we can be on our way."

I forced myself to eat some breakfast, a few nuts and some pieces of fruit, and was surprised to find that I was actually hungry. Then I realized that it had been more than a day since I had last eaten anything.

After breakfast Talos and I fed and watered the horse and harnessed her to the cart, then we packed the tent away and put everything onto the back of the cart. That done, I climbed into the back while Talos and Pentheus took their places on the seat at the front.

During all this, the section of Roman soldiers who would be travelling with us had formed into ranks in front of and behind the cart: six men across, with the officer in charge at the front.

I noticed that Simeon was in the front row of the soldiers following behind our cart, and as I looked at him he gave me a scowl. It was as I thought: he was determined to take his vengeance on me if he got an opportunity.

Pentheus flicked the reins and the horse began to amble forward, pulling the cart after it with a jerk, and then we were rolling, the soldiers' boots slamming down on the ground as they marched, while the officer in charge shouted out the beat for them to march to: "*Sinister! Dexter! Sinister! Dexter!*", which I had discovered were the words the Romans used for "Left! Right! Left! Right!"

Behind us we left yet another party of Roman soldiers laying the section of road: digging the trench, hauling stones, banging them into place. We also left the dead from the battle: the British warriors hung from trees, and the Roman soldiers buried in graves marked with stone headstones. I saw the gravestones from a distance and noticed that someone had left a small bunch of flowers on top of one. I knew that must be the grave of Asras, and that the flowers had been left there by Simeon. I looked again at Simeon, trying to read the expression on his face, but there was none. Like the rest of the soldiers he looked straight ahead, his face and eyes blank as he marched, wearing a full weight of armour, his pack on his back, along with his spears and sword, a shovel, a leather satchel of food rations; everything a soldier needed to survive for three days.

He must hate me very much, I thought. He must hate us Britons. He must hate being here in this country. I wondered where he was from. Pentheus had said the Roman army was made up of soldiers from many different countries. I wondered if Simeon and Asras were from a conquered country, given the choice to join the army or die; or had they volunteered? But most of all I wondered: when was he going to try to kill me?

Chapter XVII

For the next few days life continued in much the same way as it had done for the past weeks: a stretch of road was marked out under Pentheus's direction and construction of it began. As soon as a party of soldiers joined us after working on an earlier part of the road, our cart set off again with these new men marching with us, ready to mark out and build the next section. I noticed that Simeon and his group of eight were never far from our cart. Whether Simeon had persuaded his comrades to volunteer to keep marching rather than digging, or whether it was the way the system worked, I didn't know. All I knew was that Simeon was always there. My guess was that he was so consumed with hatred for me over what had happened to his brother that he was still intent on killing me as the nearest Briton to hand.

For my part, I believed that he was the deliverer of my punishment from the gods and that some time soon he would kill me. It was my fate. Even though I knew my punishment was expected, I still could not help worrying about it. I wanted to have courage and die bravely when

Simeon finally found a way to kill me. I didn't say any of this to Pentheus and Talos because I thought Pentheus would just dismiss it or mock me for my beliefs.

I had gone back to sleeping in the tent at night with Pentheus and Talos, and joining them for meals. Now I knew what my punishment was to be, I no longer needed to punish myself or stay out in the open and wait for it to happen.

By the morning of the twenty-eighth day, twenty-six miles of road had been constructed and we stood and watched the soldiers building the second fort.

"Fourteen miles of road to go and it will be all over," said Pentheus. "It has been a good road to build."

"It has been a bad road," I said. "It will lead to the Romans ruling us completely."

Pentheus shook his head.

"Perhaps one day the Romans will be gone," he said. "When they are, this road will still be here and your people will use it. They will say to themselves, 'This is a good road.'"

Talos nodded in agreement.

"A road is never just a road," I countered. "Nor is a fort just a fort. It's made for a purpose, and that purpose is not always for good."

Pentheus laughed.

"For one so young you are a philosopher," he said. "You

would have done well in the schools of Greece, where debate and argument are taught as a high art. Some scholars have been known to discuss the finer points of something for weeks and still never reach an agreement." He grinned. "But we are just engineers, not scholars. We don't have time to spend on lofty arguments, we have practical things to do. Like make sure the latrines work." He gestured towards the fort. "Do you want to come and check with us?"

"I thought you said the soldiers didn't need your help in building a fort?" I queried. "You said they are all built the same way."

"And they are," agreed Pentheus. "But now and then I like to check that the invisible things work. The hidden pipes. The wells for getting fresh water."

I followed Pentheus and Talos to where the fort was under construction. As with the previous fort, soldiers were constructing the outer defences by fixing tree trunks together in high walls, with earth piled against the timber. Inside, others were marking out areas for the buildings, such as the granary, where the grain was kept, and the commander's rooms. We arrived at one place where two long ditches were being dug. I noticed that these two ditches joined up again at one end, and then ran into another much deeper ditch, which led to a deep pit.

At the other end of the two ditches a box had been carved out of a large boulder.

"There," said Pentheus pointing to this stone box. "Water from a stream will be piped down to that stone box." Pointing to the two ditches, he explained: "Long wooden boxes will be built over those two ditches, and all the way along the tops of the wooden boxes holes will be made where the soldiers can sit and go to the toilet. The muck falls down into the ditch, and every so often the water in the stone box is released and flushes the muck away, into the deeper ditch from where it then goes into that pit."

I shook my head.

"It looks like a lot of bother just to go to the toilet," I said. "Why don't they just go out into the woods and do it, like we do?"

"Because it won't be safe for them if they leave the fort on their own," explained Pentheus. "And if they just went to the toilet inside the fort, pretty soon it would become a stinking place filled with disease. This way, the muck gets taken away by the water and put into a pit."

"It will still stink," I pointed out. "There will still be disease."

Talos shook his head, and mimed digging earth and spreading it.

"That's right, Talos." Pentheus nodded. "Every so often, the muck is covered with earth, which stops the smell."

"And what happens when the pit is full?" I asked.

"Another pit is dug and the drainage ditch is redirected to the new one. And, by the time that one is full, the muck in the old pit has been rotted down and can be dug out and used as manure. And then that pit can be used again."

He smiled.

"Trust me, Bran, it's a system that works. It's very simple. Most important of all, it stops the spread of disease. One of the reasons the Roman soldiers are stronger than nearly everyone else is because they are healthier. They keep themselves clean by bathing every day. A Roman soldier signs on in the army for twenty-five years. Many of them are forty years old when they retire. Some even older. How many of your tribe live beyond thirty years old?"

"Many!" I said, adding defiantly: "Anyway, we prefer to die in battle rather than sit around in old age doing nothing."

"And that is another reason why the Romans will beat you," said Pentheus. "The way to win a war is to get *your enemy* to die in battle, not for your own warriors to die." He looked serious, and then he added: "There has been a point in showing you this, Bran. Not simply to show you latrines, but to show you that the Romans think of everything, even down to the most hygienic way for Roman soldiers to go to the toilet. Their weapons, their armour, their discipline, their forts, their roads, their food, their water and sewage systems, everything is very carefully worked out down to the last detail. That is why they will beat you."

"You've said that before, and I tell you we will win," I replied firmly.

"No," said Pentheus equally firmly, shaking his head. "And if you try you will die and so will many of your people. And at the end the Romans will still have won, but hundreds of your people will have died for no reason. I like you, Bran. You are a good and brave person, and one day you will be king of your tribe, if you live that long. Your people will take their orders from you. If you carry on this war of resistance, you will be sentencing many of your people to death. Perhaps your whole tribe will be wiped out. When this road is finished and you go home to your own people, you must tell them what you've seen and tell them they have to submit to the Romans now, before more of your people die."

I shook my head.

"I cannot, Pentheus," I said. "We did not ask the Romans to come here. We want to be Britons, not Romans. And the Caledonians have shown the Romans can be beaten."

Pentheus sighed. "I've said before, Bran, your people

are not the Caledonians. And the Romans will beat the Caledonians, mark my words."

He turned and looked at the soldiers, hard at work constructing the fort.

"Come," he said. "We'll leave these conquerors of the world to their work. We have the rest of this road to finish."

Chapter XVIII

We journeyed onward to prepare the next stage of the road: Pentheus and Talos at the seat on the front of the cart, and me in the back, as always. I looked out at the surrounding country and thought about what Pentheus had said about the Romans, and about giving in. At one level, to the head, it made sense. The longer the battle against the Romans went on, the more Britons would die. The Romans had arrived in Britain with their legions well before my father and mother had even been born. In the time they had been here, hundreds of thousands of Britons had been killed fighting against them, including my own father. My cousins Carac, Ventius and Awyn were already on their way to Rome in chains, where they would be killed for the Romans' entertainment in the circus arena. So many of my tribespeople had died, and we still seemed to be no nearer to gaining freedom from Roman rule. This road that we were building would tighten the Roman grip on us even more. Perhaps it was better to give up the fight now, as Pentheus said. Accept Roman rule, and perhaps prosper under it, as had happened to people in other countries the Romans had conquered.

But that was the head speaking. Inside my heart my spirit cried out "No!"

We were Britons! We must not let our whole culture be crushed out of existence by these invaders. Everything we were, the way we spoke, the way we dressed, our gods and goddesses, our music, our houses, the way we prepared our food, the way we buried our dead and honoured our heroes, all of these had been our way of life for thousands of years. Our ancestors had died to work this land and make it ours. Their blood had soaked this ground as they had fought to carve out a safe place to live for future generations. They had done that for my parents, and for me, and for my children, should I survive to have any. For Aithne's children, and her children's children. We were Carvetii and Brigantes. We would not be Romans! Even if it took another hundred years, our people would come through this! Our voices and our way of life would survive!

For the next ten days we moved ever further eastwards, marking out the road as we went. Pentheus, Talos and I made camp for two nights while Pentheus marked out the next section of road, then we moved on, leaving the soldiers hard at work constructing it. And still Simeon was in the party that accompanied us, just behind our cart.

By now we were well on our way towards the river that ran down to the east coast, which would mark the end of the road. We were in territory that I had never been in before. Behind us the wide stone road stretched out into the west like a river. Thirty-five miles of road had been completed, with two timber and turf forts built at intervals along the way. Since that last attack, there had been no further attacks on the party by any British warriors, but I knew in my heart that attack had not been the last. I was sure the tribes would not allow this road to be finished.

I thought of my mother and Aithne, now so far away. Here, the Carvetii would be known only as a small tribe in the far west. I wondered if word about our progress had managed to get from the Brigantes here to my Carvetii tribe, and if that word would include the fact that a young British prince was still with the Romans. I hoped so, so that my mother would know I was still alive. So far.

By now we had left the high plains and moors and were heading down towards the flat lands of the coastal area. Our column was travelling eastwards through a long valley, with vast areas of thick forests stretching up the slopes on either side, to the north and to the south. As always, Pentheus, Talos and I were on the cart in the middle. We were halfway through the valley when I heard strange and eerie sounds coming from the forests on the ridge about a mile to our left, to the north. It was like wild animals calling to one another, or like birds cawing, but this sound was unlike any animal or bird I'd heard before. Then there came a drumming, as if something unseen was beating against the trees of the forests. The drumming sound became louder and louder, at the same time as the calls of the birds and animals, and now I could hear human voices among the calls, shouting and hooting and wailing.

At a shouted command from the officer at the front, the whole column stopped and stood to attention. Pentheus pulled the cart to a halt. The sound from the forested slopes to the north was getting louder and louder, and suddenly, out from the trees came an army. No, an army doesn't even begin to describe it: it was an enormous mass of men. It was the biggest army I had ever seen. If the Roman legion had started out with five thousand men, this was at least twice as large: ten thousand warriors, possibly more.

From this distance I could see that all were armed: holding spears or swords. Some had shields. There were also chariots appearing from between the trees; war chariots each pulled by a single horse. And all the time the noise continued, getting louder and louder, then dying down to a murmur, then rising again, as if it were a war chant.

"Caledonians," murmured Pentheus.

"They outnumber the soldiers five to one," I said, awed. "They will kill us all."

Then, from the forest-covered ridge to the south, came the sound of more wailing and yelling and banging, and even more Caledonian warriors appeared: maybe another ten thousand, banging on their shields and calling.

A chill went down my spine. Twenty thousand fierce Caledonians against just two thousand Romans. No matter how strong and well disciplined the Romans were, this was going to be a massacre.

I saw the commanding officer speak to four soldiers, who immediately threw off their packs and began to run along the road back the way we had come.

"The officer is sending for reinforcements," said Pentheus. "He has chosen the four fastest runners. One of them should get through."

"The nearest soldiers are miles behind us," I said. "It will take time for the messengers to get to them, and even longer for the reinforcements to reach us. And even if the whole legion were here, which will not happen, the Caledonians would still outnumber us by four to one."

"True," said Pentheus.

The mass of Caledonian warriors on both sides had not advanced any further down the slopes. They still stood in front of the forest to both the north and the south, calling and chanting and banging their spears against their shields and against the sides of their chariots.

The officer in command came to the cart and muttered something to Pentheus, who nodded and flicked the reins at the horse, and then began to turn our cart back the way we had come, towards the west.

"The officer in charge wants non-combatants out of the way!" he shouted to me. "That's you, me and Talos. So we're pulling back to a safe place, ready to flee if the Romans are defeated."

Pentheus urged the horse to go faster, heading back to the entrance to the valley. When we were a good distance from both the Roman force and the Caledonians, Pentheus pulled the horse to a halt.

"It is my hope the Caledonians will not bother with us," he said. "Not until after they have dealt with the Romans. And, by then, let us hope the reinforcements will have arrived."

"Reinforcements!" I exploded. "There are twenty thousand Caledonian warriors about to attack just two thousand Roman soldiers. By the time the reinforcements get here the Romans in the valley will have been massacred, and us with them!"

Pentheus shook his head.

"You are a Brigante prince, kept hostage by the Romans. The Caledonians will set you free. Or perhaps take you hostage for ransom for themselves. Either way, I believe you will be safe."

"And you and Talos?"

Talos looked at me and gave a big shrug and a deep sigh.

"Yes," sighed Pentheus. "To the Caledonians we are obviously Romans. We will be killed, unless the Romans in the valley defeat the Caledonians, or reinforcements arrive to rescue us. Sadly, this old horse will not outrun the Caledonian chariots."

A series of loud yells and howls came to our ears, and we saw that the masses of Caledonian warriors were running down both slopes towards the Romans, chariots racing and swords and spears waving. The attack had begun.

Chapter XIX

As the shouting and screaming Caledonians swarmed down from the forested ridges, I was sure they would just sweep across the Romans and destroy them. The Romans showed no signs of panic, despite being heavily outnumbered. A row of soldiers armed with slingshots stepped forward from either side of the ranks of the Roman force and faced both onslaughts of the oncoming Caledonian warriors. As I watched, each man swung his slingshot around his head fast, and then hurled the stone it contained hard and straight into the front rank of the Caledonians. The effect was devastating. The stones struck the first of the charging Caledonians and bodies tumbled down, which were trampled on by those rushing behind. Another row of soldiers stepped forward, also with slingshots fully loaded, and let loose another volley, bringing down yet more Caledonians. These volleys had killed or seriously injured many of the warriors at the front of the charge, which caused more confusion as the warriors rushing behind found themselves tripping and falling over the bodies of their fallen comrades. But still they came on, yelling war cries and waving swords and spears.

Another line of men stepped forward from the ranks of the Romans, these armed with short bows with which they let loose a hail of arrows straight into the charging Caledonians. Again, hundreds tumbled to the ground. The slopes were now littered with bodies of the warriors, but those who had survived the stones and arrows rushed onwards, yelling and screaming their chilling war cries. Altogether I guessed that more than a thousand Caledonians had been killed by slingshots and arrows. The Roman archers let fly with another hail of arrows, straight into the Caledonian hordes, and hundreds more crashed to the ground. Then as the Roman archers stepped back into the ranks, suddenly the outer ring of Romans brought their shields up, forming a wall of wood and metal. They began to spread out, gradually widening into a circle, and with every new soldier who stepped forward to make this circle wider, another shield was brought into the wall. At the same time the Romans thrust their spears forward between their shields and held them firm, and as the remaining Caledonians finally reached the Romans, they either ran at full tilt into a shield, or onto a spear point. The front rows had no chance to dodge because of the press of warriors chasing and pushing behind them.

"Outnumbered ten to one, you said, young warrior," said Pentheus beside me. "How many now?"

I shook my head in awe at the iron discipline of the Romans as they repulsed the attack.

"I don't know," I said. "Three thousand dead Caledonians?"

"Nearer four I think," said Pentheus.

"That's still eight to one," I pointed out.

"Maybe, if you count just numbers," said Pentheus. "But watch. As we saw in their practice, the Romans have formed themselves into two circles, one inside the other. That outer circle is made up of a thousand soldiers, standing tightly close together behind their wall of shields. No matter how many Caledonians there are, only a thousand of them can actually fight the Romans hand to hand."

"But as a Caledonian warrior falls, there's another to take his place," I said.

"True," agreed Pentheus. "And if a Roman soldier falls, one from the inner circle will step forward to take his place. And if that soldier dies, then the circle closes up and becomes a little smaller. The Caledonians may outnumber the Romans, but most of them are just standing behind the others waving their swords and shouting, and getting in the way."

As we stood and watched I realized that what Pentheus

said was true. Both sides were fighting bravely with no fear of dying, but while the Caledonians just attacked wildly with brute force, the Romans defended with a discipline I'd never seen in a battle before. They fought like one man, moving together in the same way at the same time, their shields opening together and spears and swords being thrust out, then the shields closing to form that tight defensive wall again. Now and then I saw a Roman soldier fall to the ground, but each time the circle of shields just closed up, as Pentheus had said. Meanwhile the Caledonians were dropping to the ground like so many swatted flies.

Suddenly a great shouting went up from among the Caledonians, a different kind of war cry, and they began to fall back from the Romans. Then they began to run, all of them fleeing, but this time in one direction, to the north, running up the slope, treading on the dead bodies of their comrades as they did so. I expected the Romans to give chase, but they remained where they were, in their circle of shields.

"They know the trick," said Pentheus. "The Caledonians want the Romans to chase after them thinking they are running away, but if they do that, once the Roman circle is broken the Caledonians will turn and attack them again, and this time they'd be able to cut them to pieces. Then it really would be a case of six men against one."

Pentheus was right. The Caledonians stopped before they reached the forest at the top of the slope and turned, looking down on the Romans. When the Romans didn't move but stayed where they were, the Caledonians began to jeer at them, shouting that they were cowards. But still the Romans stayed where they were, within their circle of shields, swords and spears poised ready for another attack.

For their part, the Caledonians stayed out of the trees and carried on calling and jeering at the Romans for a while, and then they fell silent and stood and glared, with just a few angry shouts coming from them. And then they began to beat their swords on their shields and chant again, their war cries rising and falling like songs. And when the drumming and chanting seemed to have reached their peak, once more they raced down the slope towards the Romans, whooping and yelling and roaring, swords and spears raised and waving. But this time they were running over the bodies of their fallen comrades, and on grass that was wet and slippery with blood.

As before, the soldiers armed with slingshots stepped forward and sent forth a volley of well-aimed stones, and then immediately the Roman archers took their place and let fly with a hail of arrows, bringing down more of the Caledonians. The northern slope was now looking like a butchery, with dead bodies lying everywhere.

As those Caledonians who had survived this latest burst of stones and arrows neared the Roman force, once more the Roman shields came up to form a long defensive line of wood and metal, with swords and spear points sticking out from the wall.

"They cannot win," I muttered. "The longer this goes on, the more Caledonians will die."

Even as I spoke, the Caledonians suddenly halted their advance down the slope before they reached the circle of Roman shields and began to shout and jeer again, waving their swords and spears over their heads. By now I guessed there were only about ten thousand of them left alive. Ten thousand Caledonian warriors dead to just a few hundred Roman casualties. As before, the Romans remained where they were, refusing to be drawn out from their circle to attack the Caledonians. Instead they just waited, poised for action, while the warriors shouted and cursed them from a distance. And then, the Caledonians fell silent and began to head up the slope again, every now and then a warrior turning and hurling abuse down at the Romans. But still the Romans did not move, just waited in their circle, ready in case the Caledonians attacked again.

The Caledonians disappeared into the forest at the top of the slope, and then there was silence from the forest.

Still the Romans did not move.

"They will wait," explained Pentheus. "Just in case it is a trick."

But it was no trick. After half an hour the Caledonians had not reappeared. And then there came the sound of thousands of running feet from the west, and I turned to see the Roman reinforcements arriving at a fast march, their booted soles crashing down on the new stone road. As they came in sight, there was a shouted command from within the circle of Roman soldiers, and they began to disperse and head towards the reinforcements to join up into an even stronger force. But it was not necessary. I knew in my heart the Caledonians had gone.

"Now do you see why the Romans will always win?" said Pentheus. "Two thousand Roman soldiers defeated twenty thousand of your fiercest and bravest British warriors. But fierceness and bravery aren't enough. The Roman army is a disciplined force, the most disciplined there ever has been. The Caledonians have suffered a major defeat today."

"But they will fight again," I said. "They will never stop fighting. Nor will we Carvetii."

"Then you will die, just like those ten thousand Caledonians did today," said Pentheus.

Chapter XX

After the battle, the commander ordered camp to be made. I was surprised at how quickly the Romans returned to their day-to-day business. When we Britons fought a victorious battle, the celebrations would last for many days, with ale being drunk and stories being told of the fighting, and wounds and weapons being proudly displayed. There were no such celebrations in the Roman camp. They set to work to treat their injured and make sure the camp was secure in case the Caledonians returned.

When that was done, the Romans laid out their dead ready for burial. Then they dragged the bodies of the Caledonians into large piles where they had fallen. And, unlike the previous attacks, they cut the heads off the dead Caledonians and hung them from the branches of the trees. This act was more than just sending a warning to anyone else who dared rise up against them. They knew that we Britons believe the head to be where the soul lies. That is why, after a victory, our warriors cut off the heads of our enemies and hang them from the walls of our huts. To possess the head of an enemy is to own his spirit and so become more powerful. The head of an enemy is an offering to the gods. The previous attacks had been skirmishes by comparison and had barely affected the Romans, so they had shown their contempt for their attackers by simply hanging their dead bodies from the trees to rot. The victory over the tens of thousands of Caledonians had been a major one, and the Romans meant to make sure that the Britons remembered it for a long time and took notice. By cutting off the heads of the dead Caledonians and leaving them to rot in the open air, the Romans were letting the Caledonians know that their gods were stronger than our British ones.

One question hung over me: had Simeon survived the battle? While Pentheus and Talos began to make the tent and prepare our fire for the evening, I excused myself from helping them and said I needed to be on my own to walk and think. My real reason was to walk through the camp and see if I could spot Simeon. I did think of going to where the dead Roman soldiers had been laid out to see if his body was among them, but guards had been placed near the bodies to protect them from crows, and other animals who fed on carrion, while they awaited burial. I thought the guards might get angry at a British boy walking among their dead, examining them, and chase me away.

I wandered through the Roman camp for almost an hour, but saw no sign of Simeon. No one stopped me or asked me what I was doing; all the soldiers knew about me by now and had become used to me walking free among them, even though I was a hostage.

By now evening was falling and the blanket of darkness was coming down and the fires outside the tents burnt bright red, sending sparks up into the sky. The smells of food cooking over the fires came to my nostrils, and I guessed that Pentheus and Talos would be preparing our meal. I was heading towards our tent, when a rough hand was suddenly thrown over my mouth from behind and I felt the point of a dagger dig into the skin of my back.

"Keep quiet, boy!" rasped a harsh voice in my ear. It was Simeon!

We were at the outer edge of the camp. I looked around. Everybody seemed too busy to take any notice of what was happening. Simeon released his hand from my mouth and grabbed my arm, his hard fingers digging into the flesh. I could feel the point of his dagger painfully in my back.

"Walk!" he commanded me in a savage whisper.

With his firm grip on my arm, he guided me away from the glow of the campfires. He kept walking, half dragging me along with him, his fingers biting painfully into my arm. I did

125

my best to try and show him that I was not afraid, but inside my bowels churned with the fear of what was going to happen to me. An even bigger ache inside me was the knowledge that I would never see my mother or Aithne again. I wanted to let them know how much I cared for them, and how — even at the end — I had fought for our British cause.

Ahead of us there were sentries on guard duty, but their backs were turned to us because they were watching for attacks from outside the camp. Simeon hesitated, then decided not to risk taking me past the sentries. Instead, he dragged me towards the supply wagons, which were gathered together in a dark corner of the camp.

"Don't waste my time begging for mercy!" he snapped.

"I would not lower myself to do that," I answered defiantly.

It was strange, but now that I was faced with the reality of my death, I no longer felt so sure it was the will of the gods. I had been saved from death many times on this journey: by Talos, by Pentheus, by the soldiers who had stopped Simeon from killing me before. Suddenly much of what Pentheus said made sense. Perhaps my death was not the will of the gods after all. Perhaps they had been showing me they wanted me to live. Yet they had brought me here. Or had they? Possibly not, because it was I who had come here searching for Simeon. I who had deliberately walked into his trap. I was a fool!

As this realization struck me, Simeon slashed at me with the dagger. I leapt to one side, but not quick enough. I felt a sharp pain in my arm, and then the wetness of blood.

I crouched, my eyes on the dagger, ready to dodge when he tried to strike again.

"Simeon!"

A hissed call behind him made him turn, surprised.

Standing behind him were two of his soldier friends. I was sure they were the same two who had saved me from Simeon before.

"Simeon, you must not do this!" said one urgently. "The commander will see it as treason, because the governor himself gave us this boy as our hostage. He is under our protection. Remember what we said: what happens to a legion where even the thought of treason is suspected. Decimation! Is that what you want?"

Simeon scowled, his face twisted in fury.

"What I want is Asras's death avenged!" he raged.

"It was avenged here today when we defeated the Caledonians," said the other soldier.

Simeon shook his head, raging with anger. He glared at the soldiers. "This boy is going to die. Now!"

And with that Simeon swung round towards me, his

dagger raised to plunge it into me. But, before he could, one of the soldiers leapt forward and grabbed him and pulled him back. Raging with fury, Simeon slashed at him with the dagger, cutting into his shoulder. He was just pulling the dagger back for another blow when the other soldier produced his sword and thrust it hard into Simeon's body.

Simeon stopped and staggered back, his mouth wide in astonishment. Then he crumpled to the ground, dead.

The soldier turned to me.

"Go!" he said. "Get back to the surveyor and his boy. We'll take care of this."

I stood there, stunned.

"But . . ." I began.

"Go!" he repeated urgently. "Go, or we will all be killed!"

I nodded and then began to hurry back towards the glow of the campfires. I was alive!

Chapter XXI

I arrived at the tent and found Pentheus and Talos waiting for me. Pentheus looked worried when he saw the cut on my arm.

"Talos," he said, "your medical skills are needed."

While Talos set to work to clean and dress my wound, I told them what had happened with Simeon.

"It seems to me that your gods want you alive, Bran," said Pentheus. "They seem to have forgiven you."

I shook my head.

"I do not understand it," I said. "I don't know what the gods want."

"I do not understand the ways of the gods, Bran," said Pentheus. "None of us do. Why is it that you can talk and Talos can't? Why is it that the Romans are here instead of your people conquering Rome? Life is full of mysteries. Do the gods have all the answers? I do not know. All I know is I have been given a road to build, and, it seems, the task of getting you safely back to your people afterwards. Is that right, Talos?"

Talos finished dressing my wound and nodded.

"What will they do with Simeon's body?" I asked.

"I expect they will add it to the bodies of the soldiers awaiting burial. They will tell the sentries guarding the bodies that Simeon died from wounds he received in the battle." He gestured towards the fire, and the food being kept warm beside it. "Now, I suggest we all eat. Talos and I have been waiting for your return before we began, and we are both hungry. As I am sure you are."

Indeed I was, which surprised me. I had narrowly escaped being killed by a grief-stricken soldier, had barely escaped with my life, and yet I felt hungry! It was strange.

As Talos served up the food onto the wooden platters for us, I thought about all that had happened recently. I thought about my mother and my sister, still held hostage awaiting my return. I thought about my cousins sent in chains to Rome to die in the arena. I thought about the Romans defeating the Caledonians with their huge disciplined army. I thought about the two Roman soldiers saving me from Simeon. And I thought about the massive road I had seen being built across our country, with forts springing up along it, to increase the domination of Rome over us.

"The gods have saved me for a purpose," I told them firmly. "I have a role to play. That role is to defeat the Romans and free this country from their rule. And I will fulfil it."

"Possibly," said Pentheus, handing me a wooden platter. "Until then, eat. Even warriors need food."

Chapter XXII

More than thirty years have passed since that journey I took with Pentheus and Talos. After it was over and the long wide road finished, I returned to my village and my mother and sister. I never saw Pentheus or Talos again. I believe they left Britain to carry out more building work somewhere else in the empire.

I am a parent myself now, with three children: two boys and a girl. I was tempted to call the boys Pentheus and Talos, out of respect for the two Greeks who came to mean so much to me all that time ago, but it would not have gone well with our tribe, so I gave my children British names.

Ten years ago my mother died and I became king of the Carvetii. With her dying breath she asked me to give her my pledge that I would continue to fight to overthrow the Romans and make Britain free again, and I gave her my word; but the truth is that the Romans are more powerful than ever. They have now been on our island for over a hundred years. Some British women have married Roman soldiers and had children with them, and some British warriors have even joined the Roman army as soldiers.

As I write these words, the new Roman emperor, Hadrian, has ordered high walls to be built between the forts along the line of the road that the Romans built under the direction of Pentheus. The Romans say this wall is to protect us from attacks by the Caledonian tribes to the north, but I am not so sure that is its only purpose. The Romans are digging defensive ditches along both sides of the wall, forty feet wide and twenty feet deep. These ditches they call the vallum. If they are building this wall to defend against the Caledonians in the north, why are they also digging these huge wide and deep ditches on the south side of the wall? It can only be to protect the wall from us, the Brigantes, because they distrust us and expect us to attack it. It is good to know the Romans still have fear of us in this way; it means my pledge to my mother has been kept. And, perhaps, my children will see the day when the Romans finally leave Britain.

Historical Note

Although this book is a work of fiction, it is based on historical fact.

The Romans invaded Britain under Emperor Claudius, in AD 43. At the time, Britain was already divided into different tribal areas. The tribes who lived in the region of what became the border between England and Scotland (along the line of Hadrian's Wall) were, to the south, the Brigante tribe (which included the sub-tribe of the Carvetii in the Carlisle area) and, to the north, the Novantae and Selgovae tribes. Further north were the Caledonian tribes.

Hadrian's Wall was not created as one single building work, but developed over years. Its base was the military road built by the Roman army across Britain from Carlisle (Roman name: Lugavalium) in the west to Corbridge (Roman name: Coriosopitum) in the east, a distance of about forty miles. This road was called the Stanegate, and it was begun on the orders of the governor of Britain, Agricola, in AD 84.

The road was built after the Roman army in Scotland had engaged the Caledonian tribes in a major battle in the

Highlands. The Caledonians had forced the Romans to withdraw to the narrow stretch of land between the Solway Firth and the River Tyne.

As Stanegate was built, two forts were built along it, thirteen miles apart. Over the years, more were built along the road at shorter intervals. Then smaller forts were added, both as watchtowers and temporary shelter for the troops.

In AD 122, nearly forty years after Agricola began building the Stanegate road as a line of defence, the emperor Hadrian ordered a new line of fortifications a short distance north of the Stanegate. He also ordered the two ends of this defensive line to be extended to Bowness on Solway (Roman name: Maia) on the west coast and to Wallsend (Roman name: Segudunum) on the east coast. This whole structure was known as Hadrian's Wall, and it was completed in AD 138. When it was finished it was 130 km long.

The Romans continued to rule in Britain until the beginning of the fifth century. At this time Rome came under attack from barbarian tribes in Europe. For many years there had also been bitter disagreements among the Roman people and the rulers of Rome about who the true emperor was and how the empire should be run. The result was that Rome began to fall apart as a military and political power. In about AD 435 the Roman troops in

Britain stopped being paid; and after a while many of them just left the army and drifted away. Most became part of the local communities. In most of southern Britain the people were now as much Roman as they were British. In Wales, Cornwall, Devon, Ireland and Scotland (places where the Romans had not had any major impact) the people were still basically of the Celtic tribes. Along the line of Hadrian's Wall the people were a mixture of British Celts, Romans and Romano-British.

And so the Roman Empire, which had been powerful and had dominated Britain for so many hundreds of years, died out.

The Roman Army

The Roman army was divided into **legions**. In the early years (about 300 BC) a legion was made up of about 4,200 men, known as **legionaries**. By the first century BC a legion consisted of approximately 5,000 men, and it was made up of ten **cohorts**. Each cohort was subdivided into **centuries**, with each century containing eighty men. The cohorts were organized as follows:

• The First Cohort (the *Prima Cohors*). This cohort was larger than the other cohorts. It contained ten centuries (800 men).

• Cohorts 2–10 had six centuries each (480 men per cohort).

• Each century was sub-divided further into ten **contubernia**. A *contubernium* was made up of eight men who shared the same tent, and ate and did everything together.

• The whole legion was led by a senior officer called a **legatus**.

• Each cohort was led by a junior officer known as a **tribunus militum**.

• The soldier in charge of each century of eighty men was known as a **centurion**.

Every legion had its own ornamental eagle, which was made of silver. It was known as an **aquila** and was carried into battle by a soldier known as an **aquilifer**. The legion's eagle was its most important symbol, and if the eagle was captured in battle by the enemy, then the legion was disbanded.

Each century had its own emblem, known as a standard, and the soldier who carried it was known as the **signifer**. The signifer also organized the money for the century's burial club, which the soldiers paid into so that if they died they would have a good funeral.

Each legion also had a back-up force known as an **auxilia**. The men who served in this were known as **auxiliaries** and were non-Roman citizens, usually from the provinces. The cohorts in an auxilia consisted of between 500 and 1,000 men. The soldiers in an auxilia were paid less than Roman legionaries and served in the army for a longer term. However, at the end of their term of military service they became Roman citizens.

When a man signed on as a soldier it was originally for a term of twenty years. By AD 5 the minimum term of service had become twenty-five years.

The Roman army on the march building a road:

A legion on the march was well-organized. If cavalry were being used, they were at the front of the column. If not, the infantry were at the front, followed by the engineers and surveyors. Behind them came the men who would build the road. Then came the carts and wagons with supplies. Next came the commander with his bodyguard, then the legion carrying their standards, with their centurions behind them. Depending on the purpose of the march, they might also have a mule train following behind carrying baggage, and finally a strong contingent of infantry and possibly cavalry to protect the rear of the column.

Roman religion

The Romans based much of their religion on that of the Greeks, and they gave the various Greek gods and goddesses Roman names to make them their own, as can be seen from the following:

Jupiter (Greek name: Zeus): king of the gods
Juno (Greek name: Hera): wife (and also sister) of Jupiter
Neptune (Greek name: Poseidon): god of the sea
Dis (Greek name: Pluto): god of the Underworld
Ceres (Greek name: Demeter): goddess of agriculture
Vesta (Greek name: Hestia): goddess of the home
Vulcan (Greek name: Hephaestus): god of blacksmiths and craftspeople
Mars (Greek Name: Ares): god of war
Diana (Greek name: Artemis): goddess of hunting and the moon
Minerva (Greek name: Athena): goddess of war and craft
Mercury (Greek name: Hermes): Jupiter's messenger
Bacchus (Greek name: Dionysus): god of feasting and wine

Among the Roman army, there was a separate religion that was a favourite of soldiers. This was Mithraism, the worship of the god Mithras, which had begun in Persia. Why this particular religion became so popular among the soldiers of the Roman army is not really clear. Perhaps it was the basic principle of the Mithraic religion: that all men were equal, whether they were slaves or senators. Lowly soldiers were fed up with always being reminded by their officers that they were at the bottom of the social order and with being beaten and fined and having their wages being taken to pay for their food. What we do know is that wherever excavations have revealed the remains of a Roman military fort or camp, they have also usually uncovered an altar dedicated to Mithras.

Celtic religion

The Celts celebrated four main religious festivals during the year, all of which were based on the seasons. The festival of Imbolc was celebrated on February 1, the start of the lambing season. At the beginning of May came the festival of Beltane. This festival marked the time of year when cattle — which had been kept close to the farm over winter and fed on hay — could be sent out into the fields to graze. In August, when the crops began to ripen and could soon be harvested, came the festival of Lughnasa. And on November 1 came the final festival, Samhain, which marked the end of the farming year when the harvest was in and the cattle were brought back from the fields.

The heart of Celtic religion was found in Ireland, and its gods and goddesses (many of which were also worshipped on northern mainland Britain) were the Dagda (the father of all gods and goddesses), Lug, Anu and Brigit. In many parts of pre-Roman Britain the Celtic gods of Wales were of prime importance, particularly the Children of the Don: Gwydion, Govannan, Nudd and Arianrod. The Celtic god Cernunnos was also an important deity.

Timeline

55 BC First invasion of Britain by Romans, led by Julius Caesar.

AD 43 Second invasion of Britain by Romans, this time led by Emperor Claudius.

AD 60 Uprising led by Queen Boudica of the Iceni against Roman occupation. In the final battle at Mancetter, a Roman force of 10,000 men (led by Governor Suetonius Paulinus) defeated Boudica's 250,000-strong British army.

AD 72 Romans arrive in the kingdom of the Brigante tribe at what is now Carlisle (in Cumbria in the northwest of Britain) and build a fort.

AD 79 Romans build a fort at Corbridge (in the northeast of Britain by the banks of the River Tyne in Northumbria). These forts at Carlisle and Corbridge are bases for their continued northward advance into Caledonia (now Scotland).

AD 83 The Romans, under the command of Governor Agricola, push northwards into the land of the Caledonians to establish their frontier along a line between the Forth and the Clyde (now the line between Glasgow and Edinburgh). The Battle of Mons Graupius (AD 83) results in 10,000 Caledonians killed against 360 Romans. But continued guerrilla attacks by the Caledonians drive the Romans back to a line between Carlisle and Corbridge.

AD **84** Agricola builds a military road linking Carlisle in the west and Corbridge in the east, called the Stanegate, constructing two more forts along the line of the road at Nether Denton and Vindolanda. This becomes the northern frontier of the Roman Empire.

AD **98** Trajan becomes emperor. He orders the construction of more forts along the Stanegate to make the frontier more secure.

AD **100** Rebellion by Brigantes, led by Argiragus, High King of the Brigantes, against the Romans. Rebellion put down.

AD **117** Brigantes revolt again. Rebellion put down.

AD **122** Emperor Hadrian orders the construction of a high wall along the line of the Stanegate to secure the frontier, extending to the sea in the west at Bowness on Solway (Maia); and to Wallsend (Segudunum) on the east coast. This will be known as Hadrian's Wall.

AD **138** Hadrian's Wall completed.

AD **139** Emperor Antoninus Pius orders the Roman army to push northwards and conquer the territory of the Caledonians and construct a new northern frontier between the Clyde and the Forth. This is the Antonine Wall. Hadrian's Wall is no longer the northern frontier of the empire.

AD **161** Brigantes rise up against the Romans again. Rebellion put down.

AD **163–180** Caledonian uprising leads to the Romans abandoning the Antonine Wall and returning south to the line of Hadrian's Wall. Hadrian's Wall is renovated to become the northern frontier of the Roman Empire once more. Further revolts in around AD 185 and AD 197.

circa AD **435** End of Roman rule in Britain. Most Roman soldiers settle in Britain with their Romano-British families; some return to Rome and continental Europe. Hadrian's Wall is abandoned.

Picture acknowledgments

P 145   Re-enactment: Roman officers, Holmes Garden Photos, Alamy.
P 146   Re-enactment: Roman soldiers marching, Chedworth Villa, Gloucs, Nick Turner, Alamy.
P 147   (**top**) Roman legionary, Caerleon, Wales, Richard Naude, Alamy.
P 147   (**bottom**) Corbridge, Hadrian's Wall, Roman soldiers using shields in defence, South West Images Scotland, Alamy.
P 148   Hadrian's Wall, towards Crag Lough, Adam Woolfit/Robert Harding Travel, Photolibrary Group.
P 149   Map and diagram by Jason Cox.
P 150   British boy by Jason Cox.

A photograph showing two members of a Roman re-enactment society dressed as Roman officers.

Roman re-enactment society members marching as Roman
soldiers.

Roman re-enactment society members running in a "Tortoise" battle formation.

At Corbridge, Hadrian's Wall: Roman re-enactment society members using their shields in a defensive formation.

A section of Hadrian's Wall.

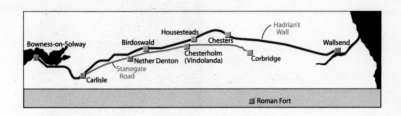

A map showing the Stanegate Roman road and Hadrian's Wall.

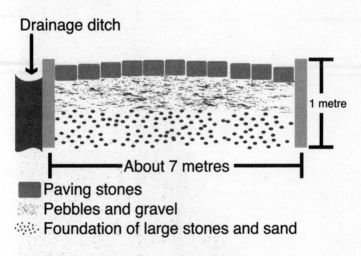

A diagram showing a cross-section of a Roman road.

149

An illustration of a British boy.